FOR SAM AND MICHAEL

CHAPTER 1: SAM & MIKEY

"Get away from there!" yelled Mrs Vala, banging on the big glass double doors leading to the outside of her apartment. "I'll wallop you if I ever get my hands on you" she screamed. Mrs Vala wouldn't lynch anyone; she was a very peaceful lady, all she liked to do was bake cakes and buy shoes, but she was desperate to get her message across, loud and clear.

Sam and Mikey jumped to attention, startled by the fist banging against the glass. As they looked back, two angry eyes stared straight at them. Glancing at each other for less than a second they took off at lightning speed, not knowing what this crazy lady would have planned for them if they stayed.

The air filled with Mrs Vala's yells, as Sam and Mikey disappeared further and further away "Don't you dare come back here! You're ruining my plants!" she shouted through the now open door.

Sam and Mikey continued for as long as they could, but having sprinted off so fast they were tiring quickly. Exhausted, they sat on a wall by the 452 bus stop and tried to regain their breath, their heads nodding back and forth, gasping for air. As they began to recover, they looked back to where that had come from. There on the ninth floor balcony of Victoria buildings stood the angry woman, still huffing and puffing, now with a large wooden broom in her hands.

"That was a lucky escape," said Mikey, turning to Sam, "they really don't like us, the people who live in these metal and glass boxes."

"I know," replied Sam "I don't understand why, and look," Sam pointed his friend towards a huge billboard that stood behind them, " I think they're going to put more of them right on top of our home."

COMING SOON: BRAND NEW 1, 2 & 3 BEDROOM APARTMENTS APPLY WITHIN.

"Where did that come from?" asked Mikey, looking at the sign. That wasn't there yesterday, he thought. Questions were buzzing around and around his head, which was wildly jerking all over the place as if looking for answers in the air. "They can't do that surely? This is OUR home, where are we supposed to live?" Mikey continued.

Sam could see his friend getting more and more anxious and needed to calm him down.

"We need to speak to my mum," he said, with a strong voice of authority, thinking that by sounding like he was in control he could calm Mikey down. "She once told me that she used to live in a lovely open space with lots of family," said Sam, "but she never mentioned it again. We need to tell her about the sign, and she can tell us about the place she used to live and we can all go there". Sam sounded less confident towards the end as he began to wonder where the rest of his family had gone, maybe they didn't like us, he thought. Luckily Mikey hadn't seemed to notice and was now much calmer.

"Let's go see your mum," said Mikey, "ooh and maybe she'll have food? I'm starving."

Sam nodded happily; it was good to see his friend getting back to normal. The fact he had mentioned food was a sign he was well and truly on the road to recovery. Sam knew how much Mikey loved his food.

So they headed off the short distance, to speak to Sam's mum and hopefully get some answers.....and bread.

Meanwhile, nine floors up, Mrs Vala was sweeping her balcony floor, trying to tidy up the mess. She inspected her pot plants closely, whilst muttering under her breath.... "stupid pigeons."

CHAPTER 2: MUM WILL HAVE THE ANSWERS

Tucked away on a ledge, between a row of garages and an unused warehouse, Mrs Major was busy cleaning, brushing away loose feathers and leaves with her tail.

Mrs Major was very glamourous. Her neck shone with the most amazing green. It glistened as the sun caught it, making it look like the most expensive emerald necklace in the world. Her slender silver body with dark grey tipped wings, was immaculately preened without a single blemish or feather out of place. The single males would constantly puff up their chests trying to impress her, but Mrs Major never showed any interest. She had and would only ever love one male, apart from her beautiful boy Sam.

Just as she was brushing off the last leaf from the ledge in rushed her little boy, grabbing her attention. He was immediately followed by his best friend.

"Mum! Mum! Mum!" cried Sam, "they're going to build boxes on our house! The lady chased us away and we saw the sign. We don't know what to do and where we are going to go and..."

Mrs Major softly unfolded her wing in front of her boy and calmly spoke. "Sam my darling, take a breath, and let's start from the very beginning."

Without taking a proper breath, Sam rushed in again. "Mikey and I were sitting on a balcony and the lady inside the box shouted at us and made us fly away and when we landed we saw the sign and..."

Again his mother interrupted, "Samuel!" she said firmly, "you're turning purple, you need to slow down and breathe."

Hearing his mum call him by his full name, something she usually only ever did when he wasn't behaving himself, he stopped and took a breath. "That's better my darling boy," she said encouragingly, "now let's start again from the beginning, but slowly this time."

Sam lowered his neck into his shoulder feathers and with big round eyes looked directly at his mother. “Sorry mum,” he said sheepishly.

“That’s ok,” she replied. She could never resist those big orange eyes; they melted her heart every time he looked at her. “Now tell me about this lady.”

Sam raised his head again and began to recount the events of earlier that morning and the sign that Mikey and him had seen.

Mrs Major listened intently as her son described the sign with the pictures of the glass and metal boxes. She remembered the exact same sign being put up before Victoria buildings had been built. There had been so much noise and dust and she had struggled every day to keep their small ledge clean. Could this really be true that their little piece of home was going to be destroyed, she thought. She would have to investigate, but for the time being there was no point in worrying the boys.

“Right then young man,” she said, “first things first, what have I told you about flying up on to the balconies?”

“Not to do it,” Sam mumbled in reply.

“The balconies are dangerous,” she continued, “what would have happened if the lady had damaged your feathers with her broom? It’s not safe for a pigeon your age to be going off on adventures. You need to stay close to home, where it’s safe. Do you understand?”

Once again Sam’s neck retreated into his shoulder feathers. “I’m sorry mum” he replied sheepishly. “We just wanted to see the view and the amazing far off places. We won’t do it again.”

“Well you don’t need to see those faraway places, you have everything you need right here,” she replied firmly, “we have this lovely ledge and we have each other and that will be the end of it.” She paused, staring directly into her son’s eyes. “Now who wants some bread, Mikey?” She turned towards Mikey whose eyes lit up at the mention of food. “I guess that’s a yes then. Now both of you go and wash your feathers and beaks before eating."

Sam and Mikey flew down off the ledge to a barrel of water which always stood at the side of the garages. Gripping onto the sides they dipped their faces into the water and flapped the water with their wings. This became more of a game than actual cleaning, as splash after splash they hit each other with water, laughing. They really were the best of friends.

When they arrived back on the ledge, water still dripping off their feathers, they saw that Mrs Major had laid out some delicious looking sandwich pieces for them both and they dived right in, pecking away at the tasty treat.

"Thank you Mrs Major," said Mikey as he devoured the last morsel "that was delicious!"

"Thank you mum," agreed Sam, "you really are the best".

Smiling to herself, Mrs Major was just beginning to turn away and start tidying again, when Mikey said something that stopped her in her tracks.

"Mrs Major," said Mikey inquisitively, "Sam tells me that you used to live in a wide open space with your family and that maybe we could all go and live there".

This had completely caught her off guard and very unusually she snapped in response. "We don't talk about that place, it's long forgotten and that's the way it should be. Now isn't it time you went back home? Your mother will be wondering where you are." Turning to her son she continued. "Sam, see Mikey home please, and come straight back."

Sam and Mikey looked at each other in shock. They had never seen Sam's mum act that way before. Mikey said thank you once again and the boys started to walk the length of the garage roof, where Mikey lived on the opposite end.

"That was odd," said Mikey, as they walked along the roof, "I've never seen your mum like that before."

“I know,” replied Sam, “I wonder why she doesn’t want to talk about her old home? We need to work out what to do and if mum’s not going to help, we need to find someone who can.”

“What we need,” said Mikey, “is someone else who might know about this place, someone older who might have also lived there.”

Suddenly Sam stopped walking and turned to his friend. “I’ve got it!” Sam exclaimed. “What we need is Grandad.”

CHAPTER 3: WHAT WE NEED IS GRANDAD

Grandad Major, or Mad Frog Charlie, as the other animals in his neighbourhood called him, due to the fact they thought he was as mad as a box of frogs, lived a quarter of a mile from the garages on the corrugated plastic roof of the bike sheds in Saint Cecilia middle school. He looked as if he had seen better days. His entire body of dark grey, almost black feathers was covered in white crusty patches, with small, odd feathers poking out from his wings and tail. His once pink feet now looked as if he was wearing big, white snow boots. On closer inspection, it turned out they were entirely covered in bird poo.

Charlie lived alone. He spent most of his time either sleeping, or watching the human children playing football during their breaks from lessons. He had to watch, because on more than one occasion their football had ended up on his roof and almost knocked him off and onto the ground.

But today was a Sunday and the school yard was quiet and Charlie was peacefully nodding his head in and out of sleep.

That morning Sam and Mikey had told their mothers that they were going to play by the garages, promising not to go near the balconies. Instead they had set off early for St Cecelia School to find and question Sam's grandad. Sam hadn't seen his grandad in a very long time but surprisingly still remembered the way; they arrived just as the sun was peaking up above the school hall clock.

Charlie's eyes opened after yet another nap and in the blur he could see what looked like two young pigeons hopping along the corrugated roof from one raised surface to the next. As his vision finally cleared he was shocked to see his grandson Sam joined by another young pigeon.

"Hello Grandad," said Sam, "How are you? This is my best friend Mikey."

"What are you boys doing here?" questioned Grandad, "where's your mother?" his head twitching in all directions looking around for his daughter whom he hadn't seen in such a long time. His heart suddenly filled with disappointment not seeing her anywhere.

"She's not here Grandad," said Sam, "we came to see you on our own as we want to ask you some questions. I hope you don't mind?"

Charlie looked at his grandson with his smart silver grey feathers and black wing tips and was reminded of his daughter. "Mind?" he said "why would I mind? It's great to see you!" turning to the other young pigeon next to Sam, "and a pleasure to meet you too Mikey. Any friend of Sam's is welcome here. Now what are these questions you wanted to ask me?"

Sam began, "Well Grandad, we were wondering about the place you used to live with mum before I was born. The place with lots of space and all your big family living in the same place. Can you tell us about it?"

Charlie was a little bemused "Why do you want to know about that place Sam? What has your mother told you?"

“She won’t tell us anything,” Sam replied.

“And we were wondering if we could move there?” interrupted Mikey “as they’re going to knock down our home and we’ll have no place to live.”

“They’re going to knock down what?” Charlie exclaimed.

“There’s a sign gone up by our home and they are going to build those glass and metal boxes for the humans on it,” explained Sam, “and I remembered hearing stories about the open space you used to live in and thought we could live there. Mum told us not to talk about it and we don’t know what to do.”

“Well I’ll tell you about it boys” said Grandad “but I don’t think it’s going to help. That was a long time ago and we can’t live there anymore.”

The two young pigeons huddled up either side of Charlie and he began to tell them the story.

“Well lads,” Charlie began, “It was many years ago and there was this wonderful place, were we all used to live. It was a big open square in the centre of London. It had two grand levels. The lower level had two huge pools of clear blue water for drinking and washing and playing, and they had fountains that would spray water all over you in a perfect shower. The upper level had the perfect ledge to rest on and stood right in front of The National Gallery. A huge building with great columns and when you looked in the windows you could see the most amazing statues. I know some of my friends back then who used to sneak inside the revolving doors and try and rest on these beautiful pieces of marble stone." Charlie chuckled to himself as fond old memories came flooding back into his brain. He could picture, as if it was yesterday, his pals going round and round in the revolving doors being chased by men in funny hats with stripes on their dark blue uniforms trying to get them out of the building and away from the statues.

"All around the square," Charlie continued, "were huge buildings and even a church with a fantastic spire, with so many ledges everywhere it made the perfect place for us all to live with all our family and friends in one place. Trafalgar Square was wonderful and it was our home."

"Trafalgar Square? Is that what the place was called? It sounds so amazing Grandad," said Sam smiling.

"Yes it was Sam, but that wasn't the best part boys," Charlie continued, "at the bottom of the square stood the most amazing column. At the bottom were four stone plinths with giant, regal looking lions on top of each of them. Each lion was as black as night and you could perch on the top of their manes and look down at the busy street below with all the big red buses and black taxis driving around day and night. Then, in the centre of the lions, was the column. It was so tall it seemed to stretch up to the sky forever and the strange thing was that right at the very top stood a man."

"A man?" exclaimed Mikey, "how did a man get up there? Did he live there?" The young pigeons looked at each other very confused.

"No boys, not a real man," explained Charlie, "this was a statue of a very important looking man whose name was Nelson. He wore a very smart uniform and a wide, triangle shaped hat and carried a sword. The strange thing was he only had one arm and his right jacket sleeve was pinned to the front of his coat. I have no idea why. But he would look down over our home and it was like he was looking after us. Watching out for danger and keeping us safe. The best bit was if you were brave enough and strong enough to fly right up to the top and sit on his hat you could see the most wonderful views of London. You could see all the way down to Buckingham Palace, where The Queen lives and St James' Park in front, were we used to go and fly around. Your mother used to love the park Sam, she used to fly around the edge of the lakes and then go and watch the horses at horse guard's parade. That's where she met your father."

"My dad?" said Sam "My dad lived there too? What happened and why didn't he come to live with us at the garages?"

Charlie had realised he had probably said too much. He could see Sam's excitement of hearing about his father but this was not his story to tell. "That's not for me to say Sam. That story is up to your mother. The only thing I can tell you is that they were both so happy there, especially when your mum became pregnant with you. Your dad would fly to the park and pick yellow daffodil heads and bring them back to the square for your mother as she couldn't fly to the park herself. But you'll need to ask her the rest yourself."

Sam was disappointed. He had finally heard about his father and had so many questions but he could tell from his grandad's tone he was not going to hear anymore from him. Sensing the tension in the air and that his best friend was getting upset Mikey piped up.

"Why don't we all still live there Mr Major?" Mikey asked, "it sounds so wonderful, why did you all decide to leave?"

"Well that was not our choice," Charlie replied. His tone had changed to one of sadness. "I don't know what really happened. The humans used to love us there. They used to come and feed us with bread and seeds. People would set up stalls around the outside of the square selling bags of seeds to the other humans so they could come and feed us. We loved it. We would come and gather at their feet and even rest on their arms and eat straight from their hands. Everyone was happy. Children would run around with their arms outstretched as we flew off around them, pretending they were flying with us too. There was one particular lady who was always there, Mrs Bread we called her. She would arrive first thing in the morning and not leave until it had been dark for hours. She would fill her coat pockets with seed, even the rim of her hat and we would all come and rest on her and eat and she would talk to us all just like friends. At some points you couldn't even see her beneath a huge standing human shape of pigeons. She always carried a plastic bread bag filled with torn up small pieces of bread which she used to scatter on the ground, that's how she got her name.

Then one day we had heard a rumour that a group of people, who lived in the grand building on the river with the tall clock tower, had decided that they didn't want us crowding up the square. We had never seen these people before and they certainly weren't the happy smiley faces we had been used to. They turned up in their dark black cars and dressed in their dark black suits and were talking to a man dressed in a tweed jacket wearing a flat cap and a big funny glove. It was then that we first met Harris."

"Who's Harris?" said Mikey, "is he another pigeon?"

"No Mikey," Charlie replied, "Harris was a young hawk"

"A HAWK!" exclaimed both boys at once

"Yes" said Charlie, "the humans had brought him from far away in the countryside and the moment he arrived things would never be the same again." Charlie paused. If the boys hadn't been mistaken they were sure they could see tears begin to develop in his eyes, but before they could fall Charlie continued his story. "At first," Charlie continued, "Harris would fly into groups of us with his sharp talons showing. We would scatter to the surrounding buildings and hide behind whatever columns or ledges we could find. Harris would then return to the roof of The National Gallery where he would look out over the square and at any sign of us he would swoop in again talons showing."

The two young pigeons looked at each other almost fearful and as if expecting Harris to appear out of nowhere began bobbing their heads around scanning the surroundings. Safe that the area was clear they turned their attention back to Grandad who continued with the story.

"This would happen day after day," said Charlie, "it was only in the evenings, when the man in the tweed jacket would return and take Harris away, that we could return to the square and eat and be with our families. There was less and less food as the people who usually fed us disappeared when we weren't there. Only Mrs Bread remained and tried to feed as many of us as she could. Gradually families began to leave the square and spread all over London further and further away from Trafalgar Square and Harris. Soon there were no families left and with lack of space some families even had to split up just to survive. That is how we ended up all the way out here." Charlie bowed his head. He had finished his story, well the bits that were his to tell anyway.

Sam and Mikey couldn't believe that what had started as such a happy tale had ended up so sad.

"That's not fair," said Sam, "if that was your home and people liked you why did they make you move? Those people in the black cars sound like bullies and Harris sounds like the biggest bully of them all." Mikey nodded in agreement next to his best friend. "Well now these people want to make us move from our home and I don't think that's fair. We should get our open space back and not let the bullies win."

Charlie looked at his grandson and smiled. He was reminded of himself at Sam's age but now he was old and tired and wasn't sure he had the energy to move again. "It's not that easy," said Charlie. "Trafalgar Square is in the past and we can never go back there."

"Well I think you're wrong!" replied Sam firmly, "I think we need to take back our home and I'm not going to stop till we do!"

"Hear! Hear!" agreed Mikey.

Charlie couldn't believe he was thinking what he was thinking. This idea was crazy. Then again he wasn't called Mad Frog Charlie for nothing. "OK boys, I'm in!" he exclaimed.

"Well then Grandad," said Sam firmly. "What we need is a plan!"

CHAPTER 4: THE PLAN

"First things first," said Sam, "we need to get the message out. We need to let all our friends and families know that we are heading back to Trafalgar Square."

"And how do you intend to do that?" asked Charlie.

"We ask the other birds for help," replied Sam. "Every sparrow, magpie and robin we know. We ask them to tell every pigeon they meet and they can tell every other bird they meet and in no time every pigeon in London will know of our plan." Sam's head turned to Mikey looking for encouragement and back to his grandad. "What do you think?" he asked. "Ok" said Charlie, "but I can think of a few problems with this plan. Firstly how are you going to know that all the pigeons want to go to Trafalgar square and will turn up to help?"

This time Mikey spoke up. "We tell them all to meet us a week from today, in the park near the square you told us about. That way we know how many people are interested before we head to the Square the following day; and of course they'll come. If we describe it to them like you did, why would they not?" Now it was Mikey's turn to look at his friend for back-up. "That's a great idea" agreed Sam. "Is a week a long enough time to get there Grandad?" he asked. "It should take two or three days I reckon and we need to get the message out, so a week should do just fine," replied Charlie. "But there's still more problems I'm afraid boys. What do you plan to do if the men bring in a hawk like Harris?"

Sam was about to speak and then paused. He had no idea what to do. He'd never seen a hawk in real life and didn't know how to stop one, but he was determined to make this work. He took a deep breath and looked his grandad straight in the eyes. "I don't know Grandad," he said, "but I will. We will find a way and we will get our home back, hawk or no hawk." Charlie looked at his grandson. He loved his confidence, again he saw his younger self and smiled. "Ok we'll get a plan for the hawk," agreed Charlie. "There's just one last problem, and this is the biggest one of all." "What's that?" asked Sam.

Charlie looked Sam straight in the eyes and said "How do you intend to convince your mother?"

Sam looked crest fallen. He'd forgotten about his mum. She didn't want to talk about Trafalgar Square, so why would she want to go there? If only he knew why she didn't like the place, but Grandad wasn't going to tell him. He was the only person who knew why she didn't want to talk and who might be able to change her mind.

"Grandad, I think I might need your help with that," said Sam.

Back at the Victoria Building garages Sam's mother was meeting up with Mrs Hedges, Mikey's mum, to go and find some food. As they rounded the corner by the 452 bus stop Mrs Hedges spotted an open packet of crisps. Flying over she noticed that inside were 2 untouched snacks which would make the perfect snack for the boys when they got back from playing together. She turned around to ask her friend to carry one back to the garages for her and was shocked to see her friend standing absolutely frozen, with her beak wide open.

"What's wrong Lizzie?" Mrs Hedges asked. "You look like you've seen a ghost."

Mrs Major didn't speak, she just raised a wing and pointed directly above her friends head. Mrs Hedges turned around and looked up to see the huge billboard advertising new apartments to buy that were to be newly built on the site.

"Jackie," Mrs Major finally spoke. "The boys were right, they are going to knock down our homes. What are we going to do? We are going to have to find somewhere else to live."

Mrs Hedge's dropped the potato crisp she was holding in her mouth and flew straight over to her friend. "This is awful Lizzie," she said. "I can't believe this is happening. But we have to stay strong for the young ones and get our thinking caps on. I'm sure an opportunity will present itself and we'll just have to take it and start again". "You're absolutely right," replied Mrs Major, "something will come up, I know it will."

At that exact moment round the corner came Sam & Mikey and it looked like someone else was with them.

It couldn't be, thought Mrs Major. It just couldn't. But it was.

"What are you doing here?" said Mrs Major angrily "and why are you with the boys? I told you I never wanted to see you again."

"Well that's a nice way to greet your father after all these years," replied Charlie, "the boys came and saw me and they've asked for my help".

Mrs Major jerked her head quickly in the direction of her son with a glare. "Is this true, what could you possibly want from him?"

"Yes Mum, it's true," replied Sam sheepishly. "Mikey and I are worried about where we are going to live and we wanted help. So we asked Grandad about where you used to live in

Trafalgar Square and we think we should go back and live there, we've even made a plan."

"Trafalgar Square? A plan?" Mrs Major's voice was getting louder and the green necklace around her neck seemed to be turning red. "What has that man been telling you? We are absolutely NOT going back to that place. I bet he didn't tell you the whole truth, did he? I bet he didn't tell you that's where your father died when I was still pregnant with you, Eh? And I most certainly can guess that he didn't tell you that it was all HIS fault!" Mrs Major suddenly burst into uncontrollable tears and flew off back in the direction of the garages and the safety of her ledge.

"Grandad, is that true?" asked Sam, his voice beginning to crack as his eyes filled up with tears. "Are you the reason my Dad died?"

"Sam, my dear boy, I promise it was not my fault," said Charlie.

"Why would Mum lie?" replied Sam crying as he did.

"I promise I will explain what happened but for the time being I must go and speak with your mother. Ok? Stay here with Mrs Hedges for just a little while and we will have a proper talk later." At that point he flew of in the same direction as his daughter, leaving Sam and Mikey stunned at what they had just heard. Mrs Hedges flew over to the boys and with two outstretched wings hugged them both close to her chest.

Mrs Major was sat huddled in the corner of the ledge when Charlie arrived. Her uncontrolled sobbing had subsided but tears still ran down her cheek and neck, which now glistened even brighter green, as the droplets of tears shone in the sunlight.

"Lizzie," said Charlie quietly, "Lizzie, can we talk?" There was silence. Mrs Major didn't move a muscle. "We really need to talk my darling," he continued. "I can understand that it's a shock to suddenly see me, and I was just as shocked when the boys came to visit, but it's happened and we need to talk it through." He noticed a slight wobble in her stillness so continued. “Isaac made me promise to go with you. He made me promise to keep you safe. You were too heavily pregnant to fly far distances and he wanted someone he could trust to be with you and look after you and his baby.” Charlie paused he could see his daughters head bowing slowly. He desperately wanted to go and give her the biggest of hugs but he had to finish what he had to say. “If I had ever known,” he continued, “if I had ever thought for one moment that Isaac wouldn’t make it after us, I would never have left him in the Square. If I could turn back time and swap my place for his I would do it in a heartbeat.” Charlie’s eyes blurred with tears. He hadn’t noticed that his daughter had turned around and was slowly making her way toward him. It wasn’t until he felt her soft silver wings around his shoulders that he knew she was there. Together as one, neither of them spoke; they just gently sobbed into each other shoulders.

After a few minutes Mrs Major lifted her head and looking straight into her father’s eyes said “I’m sorry Dad.” Charlie smiled and gave his daughter another big hug.

"Dad, I understand that it was not your fault," said Mrs Major, "but why would you convince the boys to go back to Trafalgar Square, with that horrid hawk and everything that happened why would you want them to be at risk?" Mrs Major's face was no longer one of sadness but now puzzlement.

"It was their idea Lizzie darling. It had nothing to do with me at all. I told them exactly what the men and the hawk did, without mentioning Isaac, and they still think we should go back and take all the pigeons with us. You've obviously raised a very brave and determined young pigeon because he wants to stand up to the bullies and get our rightful home back. They've even devised a plan."

"That boy is getting more and more like his father every day," said Mrs Major. "Well I guess I better hear this plan of theirs and I guess it's about time he knew the truth about his father. Thank you Dad, I'm sorry it's been so long."

“Don’t worry darling,” replied Charlie, “now let’s go and get the others, I’m sure they’re wondering what on earth is going on

For the next few hours Mrs Major, Sam and his grandad talked and talked about the past, Sam’s father Isaac, Trafalgar Square and the plan to get their home back. Mikey and his mother listened intently and agreed to come along too.

“We must come up with a way to deal with that horrid hawk before we get near the square,” Mrs Major said firmly, “it has to be our top priority, so all get thinking.”

“Does anyone know which way Trafalgar Square is?” asked Mrs Hedges “I’ve been here so long I don’t have a clue, all I remember was it was close to The London Eye that the humans built on the river, but why they called it an eye I will never understand, when it looks like a big bicycle wheel.”

“Bicycle Wheel?” asked Sam, “well I know exactly where that is.”

"How can you know that?" questioned his mother.

"I can see it from the crazy lady's balcony on the 9th floor," Sam replied, "Mikey and I can show you."

So with that the five pigeons flew up to the 9th floor balcony and looked out across the surrounding suburbs and towards the City and faintly in the distance, the boys were right, you could see The London Eye.

"Right then!" said Mrs Major, "tonight Jackie and I will spread the word around the neighbourhood and speak with all the other birds too. Dad, you look after the boys and in the morning we start heading east. Agreed?" She looked around at the others and held her right wing out in front of her. One by one they all stretched out their right wings, one on top of the other and in unison raised them into the air shouting "Agreed!"

Suddenly at the window appeared an angry red faced woman. She quickly turned around and grabbed her broom which was still standing nearby. She turned back towards the glass but to her surprise all she could see was sky.

Down below the balcony, flying through the air Mrs Major turned her head towards her son and said, “she really is a crazy lady,” and then they both started laughing and continued all the way back to the garage ledge.

CHAPTER 5: A FINE DAY FOR FLYING

Early in morning, five days after the plan was hatched, the five pigeons gathered on the top of the garages, ready to depart on their epic journey.

The previous four nights, Mrs Major and Mrs Hedges had travelled the entire neighbourhood, speaking to every pigeon that they could find, to tell them of their plan. Some had thought they were crazy to attempt it; some were too young to have any memories of Trafalgar Square but, after listening to the passionate plea that Mrs Major made, the majority agreed it was time to get their home back.

With the help of robins, sparrows, blackbirds and even one magpie, the plan was spread. The magpie helping was odd, they thought, as magpies and pigeons didn't usually get on, perhaps he saw it as an opportunity for all the pigeons to leave his patch, or maybe he was just a nice magpie, either way they were grateful for his help.

The news travelled, far and wide, that every pigeon should meet in St James' Park, opposite Clarence House, that Saturday.

The mum's had chosen Clarence House as all the older pigeons would know exactly where it was. Prince Charles who lived there was so kind to all the birds, often feeding them the bread from his kitchens and chatting to them from his windows. No pigeon forgot that bread; it was the best bread you could ever eat.

"Right everyone!" exclaimed Charlie, "are we ready to do this?" He looked around the group to see nothing but smiling faces.

"You bet!" shouted Sam.

"Let's go!" cheered Mikey

Both mums looked at each other with pride but also a little worry. "Right lads! Ground rules!" said Mrs Major sternly. "You ALWAYS fly in formation. Grandad will be at the front, you boys either side of him and me and your mother, Mikey, on the outsides. Got it?"

"Yes Mum/Mrs Major," said both boys simultaneously.

"Right then," Mrs Major continued, "I guess it's time, on three, we go."

All together the group started counting, "1...2...3", and with a flurry of flapping wings, which sounded like a helicopter taking off, they took to the sky.

They quickly got into the agreed formation and with a flying visit to the crazy ladies balcony to check directions, they started flying east.

Sam whispered to himself, "Trafalgar Square here we come."

It was a perfect day for flying. The sun was shining brightly in the sky and there was a good wind, so that it wasn't too much effort. The five of them flew high above the houses, which looked so small that Sam and Mikey felt like giants.

After a short while Charlie spotted two big lakes of water. He turned his head left and gestured towards the ground with his wing.

“Looks like a good place to take a break?” He shouted, so he was heard above the wind.

“Good idea,” replied Mrs Major. “Right everyone let’s head to the lake on the left.”

With that Charlie changed the direction of the formation and headed towards the ground. As they got closer they could make out a sign: THE QUEEN MOTHER RESEVOIR. Suddenly, distracted by the sign, and just about to touch down on the ground Mikey flew directly into a plastic bag that had been thrown up by a sudden gust of wind.

Trapped inside, Mikey flapped like crazy. “Help!” he yelled “I can’t.....” and with that, he hit the ground, rolling along the edge of the reservoir for several metres, wrapped in white plastic.

“Mikey!” screamed his mother. “Don’t move! I’m coming!” Mrs Hedges flew as fast as she could and began pulling at the plastic with all her might. Every time she pulled at the bag it seemed to cover him further, but she continued again and again desperately trying to free her boy.

"Wait!" shouted Sam "I know what to do." He directed Mrs Hedges to grab the white handle attached to the bag. He then moved to the other side and grabbed the opposite handle with his beak. "Now walk backwards slowly," he told Mrs Hedges.

"Stay still Mikey, you'll be free in no time," he reassured his best friend. As if by magic as they pulled on the handles, it opened a wide hole in the top of the bag. As soon as he could Mikey crawled out of the gap and was covered by the wings of his mother giving him a big, strong hug.

"Are you ok my darling?" she asked, "are you hurt?"

"I'm fine Mum," replied Mikey in his bravest sounding voice. He wrestled himself from his mother's wings and hopped over to Sam, giving his friend the biggest smile. "Thank you matey, I thought I was a goner for a second; but don't tell my mum that," he winked.

“Well done Sam,” said Mrs Major, now by his side, “that was very clever of you and do you know what? You may have just given me an idea.” She then kissed her son on the cheek and wandered over to Charlie.

After about an hour, with Mikey fully recovered and everyone’s thirst quenched from the water, it was time to move on. In no time they were back in the air and in formation. It wasn’t long however before they could all hear a really loud whirring noise coming from up ahead, louder than anything they had ever heard before.

Once again they made their way toward the ground, landing at the edge of a chain link fence surrounding a huge area of ground. The noise seemed to be coming from the other side of the fence. It got louder and louder and then suddenly disappeared, starting again minutes later.

At that moment they were all thinking the exact same things. What was this place? What were those noises? And most importantly, was it safe to go across?

CHAPTER 6: THE MACHINES

The five pigeons poked their heads through the bottom of the chain link fence and scanned the area. Over to the right was a gigantic building made entirely of glass that looked like a giant greenhouse. In the distance two more, smaller greenhouses glistened in the sun. Ahead of them, surrounded by grass was a long, straight strip of road, but this was much bigger than any road they had ever seen.

Surrounding the three greenhouses Sam could see what looked like giant white birds; but these were like no birds Sam had ever seen before. They had huge wings, a strange blue belly and a tail that pointed straight up, brightly coloured in red, white and blue.

At that moment one of the creatures started to move backwards away from the greenhouse. It then turned and headed towards the huge road, making a low whirring sound as it went. The huge white body stopped at the end of the road and fell silent.

All of a sudden the loud noise returned, deafening the watching pigeons. Then out of the blue it shot forward and headed down the road. Halfway down it took to the air, climbing quickly and steeply into the sky and within what seemed like seconds, it was a just a small dot far in the distance, before it disappeared.

"I don't think that's a bird," said Mrs Hedges. "I think it's some sort of machine. Look beneath the wings, those tubes have rotors inside and that's what's making the noise".

"Well whatever they are," said Charlie, "we need to get to the other end of that huge road, so we better be careful and watch out for them. Let's get a move on."

The five of them removed their heads from under the fence and with a flurry of flapping wings lifted up and over to the other side, stopping on the grass just short of the road. Meanwhile another of the white bird machines had moved away from the greenhouse and was once again heading towards the road where it stopped, just like the one before.

"We better wait here," said Mrs Major, "and get a closer look".

Again the great noise came, but this time the pigeons could also feel a breeze travelling though their feathers. As the noise got louder the breeze got stronger and stronger and suddenly without warning, Sam and Mikey were lifted off the ground and thrown through the air, back towards the fence.

"Flap your wings," shouted Charlie; but the boys just rolled over and over in the air. No matter how hard they tried they could not fly forwards. The noise got increasingly loud and soon enough, the three remaining pigeons were also rolling backwards along the grass, in the direction of the two youngsters.

Mrs Major grabbed at the grass with her feet and held on with all the strength she could muster, her wings still flapping behind her uncontrollably.

As the machine moved forward and took to the sky the wind began to lessen. Mrs Hedges and Charlie stopped rolling backwards and got back on their feet. Mrs Major was able to release her grip on the grass; but the two young boys were not so lucky. Unable to regain control they both fell directly to the ground, like two big grey stones. They landed only inches away from where they had started, right by the fence.

"We're never going to get across if that keeps happening," said Mrs Major, "maybe we should go around the outside of the fence?"

"The area's too big," replied Charlie. "It would take too long. We've got to try and time it perfectly and get down that road, otherwise we'll never reach Trafalgar Square in time."

The five of them huddled round in a circle to try and come up with a plan, deciding that they should stay by the fence and watch for a while, to see how regularly these machines came to the road.

"Maybe we can find a long enough gap to make our move," said Charlie. They all agreed and for the next ten minutes they sat and watched as the big white machines made their way to the road one after another like clockwork. Mikey and Sam counted out loud, from the time the machine left the greenhouse until they couldn't feel the wind pushing against their feathers. They would have two and a half minutes.

"Ok," said Mrs Major, "we need to get as close to the road as we can without being pushed over when the next wind starts, so we have the shortest distance to travel."

As the next machine moved down the road, the five of them moved step by step closer, stopping the moment Mikey was knocked on his tail but didn't roll further.

"This is the spot," said Mrs Major. "We'll gather our strength while one more flies off and then we go. Agreed?" she asked, and everyone agreed. "We will have to be quick," she continued and she turned to Sam and Mikey. "Boys, you will have to fly harder and faster than you ever have before. Stay low to the ground, stay in formation and whatever you do don't look back."

"Sure thing," they replied. "We can be really fast," added Mikey proudly.

They sat there nervously while the next machine trundled towards the road and stopped.

“Get ready to go,” shouted Charlie, making sure he could be heard over the sound of the machine. “I’ll count us in, and we go on three.”

As the machine moved forward they could all feel the breeze through their feathers again but with the distanced planned perfectly none of them moved an inch. It took to the air and a moment later Charlie started to shout. “1.... 2....3,” he yelled and the five pigeons took to the air simultaneously. Keeping low to the ground, they flapped their wings so fast the air around their bodies looked like a blur. In no time they reached the wide, dark black road and flew directly down its centre.

As the road stretched out far in front of them the next bird-like machine pushed back from the big glass building. All the time she couldn’t hear the softer whirring noise Mrs Major knew they were safe. She turned her head to look behind and could see the huge white body of the machine turning on to the end of the road. They had only got half way and she started to worry.

“You’re doing great boys! Really great!” she shouted. “Now let’s try even faster, the fastest you’ve ever gone.” Luckily for Mrs Major, Sam and Mikey, in the middle of the formation, couldn’t hear over the sound of their busily flapping wings, as she heard the loud whir from the tubes behind them, as the machine started to move down the road.

Charlie could see the end in sight. It wouldn’t be long until they were safely on the grass at the far end of the road.

“We’re almost there,” he shouted back to the group, “not far now”.

Mrs Major allowed herself to smile. They were going to do this, she thought to herself, but her positivity suddenly disappeared as she noticed Sam and Mikey slowing down and raising higher into the sky.

"What's happening?" shouted Sam. "Something's pulling me".

"Me too," shouted Mikey worriedly.

"It's just the wind," responded Mrs Major quickly, "fight against it, you're almost there".

However, Sam and Mikey continued to be pulled backwards and upwards and were now out of formation behind their mothers and a metre higher than the rest. They continued to flap their wings as fast as they could but as the machine behind them got closer and closer the young pigeons were being pulled nearer and nearer to the whirring round tubes underneath its wings.

"We've got to go back," shouted Mrs Hedges "we've got to save the boys."

The two women turned, flapping their wings so they hovered in mid-air. They looked back and could see the boys struggling against the pull of the machine.

"Keep going boys, head towards the ground if you can," Mrs Hedges yelled. The young pigeons pointed their heads towards the ground but they moved neither downwards or up. It was like they were frozen in the sky.

The huge machine rose higher and higher behind them, the big blue tubes almost on top of them. Pushing all thoughts of danger to themselves out of their minds, the ladies flew straight towards their sons.

Suddenly with a big burst of energy the blue body of the machine raised even higher in the sky and as if by magic, the pull that Sam and Mikey had felt disappeared. It was as if someone who had been holding their tails had suddenly just let go. Still flapping their wings Sam and Mikey were propelled forward with increased speed that within moments they were flying past their mothers heading back towards them.

The ladies immediately turned and followed after their boys and in no time at all they had all landed safely on the grass, at the other end of the road. The pigeons collapsed with relief and exhaustion, sinking into the soft green grass.

"We made it!" exclaimed Charlie, "I can't believe we made it!" None of the others could speak; they just gazed into the sky watching, as the blue belly of the big white machine rose higher and higher, until it completely disappeared from view.

Lying in the grass off to one side, Mrs Major shed a single tear of joy. Her boy was safe and they were one step closer to Trafalgar Square. Surely the worst was now behind them. They would rest for a few minutes more, she thought, and then the journey must continue.

CHAPTER 7: A CLOSE CALL

Well rested and over their ordeal the five brave pigeons continued flying east. Passing over the roofs of red brick houses and busy roads they decided to take a break on the flat roof of a building in the centre of a car park. Deep underground they could hear a low rumbling sound. Sam and Mikey stood up on edge, their heads bobbing from left to right, as their eyes jerked in all directions looking for danger.

“It’s not the machines again?” asked Mikey worriedly, “I can’t see them, where are they?”

All of a sudden out to the side of the car park a tube train appeared from under the ground and headed away from the pigeons. Carriage after carriage appeared from underneath the car park, rattling and rumbling as it went until again it disappeared into the distance heading east.

“There you go Mikey,” said Charlie, “nothing to worry about. It’s just a tube train. That’s the rumbling noise you could hear.”

“This could be really helpful,” said Mrs Hedges. Looking off in the direction of the train she pointed, with her wing, to the long straight line of track that followed the train into the distance. “If we fly in the same direction as the track it should lead us straight into London and stop us getting lost.”

“That’s a great idea Jackie,” Mrs Major told her friend. “It should make it quicker and a lot safer. “Have we all had enough rest?” she asked the group, “there’s no time like the present.” The group nodded in agreement and taking off from the flat roof they hovered for a moment before heading towards the tracks.

Flying above the tracks was easy. There was plenty of space and the birds could fly in formation with plenty of space between them. There were no obstructions and after the eventful morning they’d had, they now seemed to be making up for lost time. As they passed through different stations the two boys began to show off to the watching and pointing humans standing on the platforms. They started with loop the loops and even flew upside down, all to the bemusement of the watching crowd who had never seen pigeons behaving this way.

"Stop showing off!" Mrs Major instructed the two boys.

"Relax," Charlie said turning towards his daughter, "let the boys have fun." Then turning to the two youngsters Charlie announced dramatically, "watch out boys, let me show you what this old pigeon can do!" With that he launched himself high into the sky, looped the loop and then headed straight towards the ground barrel rolling as he did. Pulling up at the last minute before hitting the ground Charlie suddenly became increasingly dizzy, losing concentration he hit the floor with his tail and started rolling down the railway track in front. He finally came to rest talons outstretched next to one of the wooden railway sleepers. "Woo Hoo!" he exclaimed. "That was amazing! There's life in the old pigeon yet, eh boys?" he boasted.

The rest of the group came down to rest either side of the happy but slightly out of breath old bird.

"That was brilliant," cheered Sam to his Grandad, "can you teach me to do that?" he asked excitedly.

"He most certainly will not!" interrupted Mrs Major looking disapprovingly at her father. "He could have been seriously hurt and should know better." She fixed his eyes with a firm stare and continued, "now let's get on we can rest at the station up ahead."

The pigeons took to the air in the direction of the nearby station platform roof. That is all except Charlie who remained on the track beneath them.

"Come on Dad" called back Mrs Major. "Get a move on."

"I can't," he replied, "I think my foot's trapped". He looked down towards his legs but could only see one foot. He was right, his right foot was now wedged underneath the wooden railway sleeper and no matter how much he tried he couldn't pull himself free.

"Stay in the air boys," Mrs Major instructed Sam and Mikey, "Jackie come with me." The two ladies flew down to Charlie as the young pigeons circled overhead.

Mrs Major grasped her wings around her father's body and began to pull, but it was no use, he didn't move. Moving behind her friend Mrs Hedge's used her wings to surround her friend and after a count of three they both started pulling backwards. Nothing. "Okay, what else can we try?" asked Mrs Major, at which point she heard the boys shouting up above.

"We've got a problem," shouted Mikey to the group down below. The three pigeons looked up; there Mikey and Sam were waving their wings back in the direction of the track they had just come down. "There's a train!" shouted Mikey "and it's coming this way!"

Quickly the two ladies grabbed at Charlie once again and started to pull but nothing they could do, would release his foot from under the sleeper. The sound of the train began to get louder as it rattled along the track towards them at high speed.

Sam turned to Mikey "I've got an idea," he said, "follow me." He led his friend to the ground either side of his Grandad.

"What are you doing?" asked his mother. "You need to get to safety".

"I've got an idea and we'll all need to help if it's going to work," replied Sam. At that moment the train came round the corner and hurtled towards them. "Right we need to be quick," said Sam, "we've only got one chance at this. See the stones Mikey?" His friend nodded, "we need to peck at them to get them loose." He looked at his friend and in a moment of genius said "Mikey, pretend they're bird seed. Mum, get ready to pull."

With that the two boys began pecking at the grave stones surrounding Charlie's foot and the wooden sleeper. Imagining the bird seed before him, Mikey went crazy, digging and flicking stones out of the way; suddenly Charlie could feel his foot begin to wobble. "Pull!" shouted Charlie. "Pull!" The ladies pulled with all their might and as quickly as he tumbled to the ground Charlie was released from the grip of the sleeper and they all fell backwards. As she rolled head over heels Mrs Major caught sight of the train just metres away. "Scatter!" she shouted, "NOW!" and with that the train barged through the track and over the spot where Charlie had been trapped.

Mrs Major had reached the side of the tracks just in time and looked around her quickly. No one else was there. Her chest tightened with worry and for what seemed like forever the carriages of the train rumbled passed with a deafening sound, and although she was shouting loudly for her son, she could not even hear her own voice.

As the train passed and the dust settled she immediately spied Jackie holding Mikey closely under her wing. "Sam!" she shouted "Sam, where are you?" She frantically crossed the tracks and a sudden relief passed through her body as out from a nearby blackberry bush came the heads of her father and her son. She ran over and smothered them both with her wings, pecking them both with kisses of joy and relief.

"You saved my life," said Charlie turning to his grandson, "you are such a clever and brave young pigeon," he continued. "That goes for you too Mikey", he said turning towards Sam's friend. "If I can ever get you anything, don't hesitate to ask."

"Well," Mikey replied, looking back at Charlie. "All this talk of bird seed has made me rather hungry; is there any chance you can pass me a blackberry?" He pointed to the bush behind them. He started to giggle and within moments they were all laughing and cheering! "Mikey, you shall eat like a king," said Charlie, and he headed to the bush to gather enough blackberries for everyone.

That evening they fed like royalty and chatted over the adventures of the day, on the roof of Turnham Green station. "Well I think that's enough excitement for one day," said Mrs Major. "I think we've all deserved a good night's sleep and let's pray tomorrow is a less eventful day." With that, they flew under the nearby bridge and rested on an iron beam. This would be a safe place to stop she thought and within minutes they were all fast asleep and cooing softly.

CHAPTER 8: 62 BARROWGATE ROAD

"I think we should stay away from the railway line," said Mrs Major as they sat under the bridge.

They had all been awake for some time having slept soundly. The sun was beginning to rise and a constant rumbling sound was coming, not from the railway line above, but from Mikey's stomach.

"And it sounds like we better find some food," she continued. "If we stick to near the human houses we're bound to come across something to eat and a small detour won't make that much difference."

So the group gathered themselves together and took off heading north, in search of food.

They arrived at Barrowgate Road not long after leaving the station. It was beautiful. Tree's lined both sides of the street and blossoms burst from their branches, turning the whole road various shades of pink. The terraced houses either side were made of red brick with white framed wooden windows. They each had small well-kept gardens to the front and long thin gardens to the rear.

As the pigeons flew along the rooftops they suddenly spotted a back garden full of lush planting. The edges of the garden were full of roses in every colour imaginable, and there at the far end of the garden were three hanging feeders, full to the brim with seed.

"I think we've found breakfast," said Charlie, landing on the warm tiled roof of number 62, followed closely by the others. Mikey flew off immediately towards the rear of the garden followed swiftly by his mother and then the rest of the small group of travellers. He landed on a small paved area at the rear of the property and looked up longingly at the tubes filled with seed. His mother landed on a nearby bird bath, filled with water, and started to drink, while still keeping one eye on her son.

As Mikey flew up to the first feeder he noticed a problem, which hadn't been visible from the roof. All of the tubes were surrounded by some sort of green cage. The bars of the cage were only big enough to allow someone much smaller than Mikey or the others to get through. He hovered by the feeder, flapping his wings franticly, he attempted to poke his head through the bars; but with every attempted he couldn't get anywhere near the precious food. He returned back to the ground disheartened.

"I can't get anything" he said turning to the others, "why would they put the food in a cage? It doesn't make sense."

Mrs Hedges was just about to reply when her attention was distracted by a rustling, coming from the dense leaves of the rose bush that covered the far end of the garden. Again the bush rustled, louder this time and several areas of it shook. Everyone's attention turned from

Mikey to the bush. More rustling came from deep within the bush, like something out of a scary movie, but none of the pigeons could see the source of all this movement. It must be big, because the whole bush is moving, thought Sam and then all of a sudden they could all spot the stretched neck of a creature, its head searching the air, like a velociraptor searching for its prey. But this was no dinosaur; and with that there was a flurry of leaves, noise and wings, and out of the bush came four small sparrows moving and flapping their wings so fast that the pigeons couldn't keep up with which directions they were flying until they all came to rest and stood in front of Mikey.

"Hello, I'm Timmy," said the first sparrow, "and this is Rich, Ron and Ivor" pointing down the line of sparrows to his left. "Hello," the remaining sparrows said in unison.

"Hello," replied Mikey somewhat confused by the whole situation, and he introduced himself.

"Well Mikey," said Timmy, who was obviously the leader of this gang, "the reason there's a cage around the seeds is so large birds like you can't steal OUR food. The humans put it there for us because they like us," he continued slightly smugly.

"But that's not fair," piped up Sam, "we're all birds, so what makes you so special?"

"Because the human's don't like you," replied Rich, "because you make a mess and damage their plants with your big, noisy wings." He turned to his fellow sparrows for support and continued "and you certainly don't look as cute as us."

"But they do like us," replied Sam, "and they used to feed us too, in Trafalgar Square, and we're heading there now and they will feed us again, you just wait and see."

Mrs Major stepped in, moving in front of her son to talk to the group of sparrows. "Good Morning gentlemen," she said, "we would be extremely grateful if you could help us get a little food so we could continue on our journey and leave you to your lovely garden, with our thanks." She smiled.

"No!" exclaimed Ivor, "if they spot us feeding you, the humans will take away the food and we'll have nothing and that's that," he turned his back on the pigeons. "Come on lads, let's get out of here," and in another flurry of wings the sparrows disappeared at speed, over the fence. The pigeons were surprised to see that one sparrow remained. The one, who hadn't spoken, called Ron. Still without saying a word, he flew straight up to the nearest bird feeder, slipped through the bars and using his beak as a shovel started throwing seed from the feeder to the ground below.

The pigeons pecked at the seeds on the ground until they were full and the ground was clean.

"Thank you Ron," said Mrs Major.

"Yes thanks," said Mikey, "you're a star."

Ron flew back to the ground and spoke for the first time since meeting the pigeons. "That's ok, we are all birds after all and don't mind the others, they are good guys really, they just worry a lot and know we have a good thing here."

"Well you are special," said Charlie, "and it's a shame about the others because with the speed and flying skills you guys have, you could have been helpful to us in defeating the hawk."

"A hawk?" asked Ron, "what have hawks got to do with anything?" Charlie began to tell Ron the tale of the Trafalgar Square hawk and of their plan to return there.

"Well I'll tell whoever I can," said Ron, "but don't count any Chickens with the others. We don't like hawks either because they attack small birds like us too, so I wish you all the luck in the world, you're going to need it. Now I must go and join the others before they miss me." And with that he disappeared over the fence.

"Bye!" shouted Mikey, but Ron was long gone.

"Right then everyone," said Charlie, "I think it's time our journey continued." The pigeons took off pausing on the roof to take one last look at the beautiful blossom lined street and with that they took to the air and continued eastward.

CHAPTER 9: THE QUEEN'S FOCACCIA

After flying for hours the five pigeons were beginning to tire. The residential houses had turned to larger glass office blocks and the narrow tree lined streets below had turned to wider, concrete lanes full of cars and lorries. Finally up ahead they spied several areas of green.

"That one's too big," said Charlie, "there doesn't look like any suitable places to rest with cover." Further ahead to the right he spied a green area behind a huge grand house. The whole area seemed to be surrounded by a tall dark brick wall. That would be perfect thought Charlie, very safe. "Follow me!" he called to the others and he tilted his wings turning right and down towards his chosen sanctuary.

They landed in what was a large lawn, larger than any garden lawn any of them had ever seen before. The grass was cut so short, that it felt like solid ground and strangely it seemed to be striped. Long lines of alternate green colours lead from a small lake, with an area of trees on the opposite bank, all the way up to a huge cream coloured house with elaborate columns and huge windows framed on the inside by red velvet curtains.

"This place is beautiful," said Mrs Hedges, "maybe we should just stay here?"

"I'm not sure," said Sam, "does anyone else feel like they're being watched?" They all started to look around but there was nothing else in sight; just the trees, the lake, the lawn, the house and a small grey mound just in front of the large doors into the house.

As they looked towards the house, wondering who lived there, the small grey mound became two smaller mounts, then moments later there were four and, if their eyes didn't deceive them, the mounds were getting closer. By the time they had become clear, they were only a few metres away and they were not mounds at all but ten large pigeons marching in their direction. Their feet moved in unison, left together, right together and as they got closer the central pigeon could be heard saying "left, right, left, right, left right" and as they arrived in front of Sam and the others he shouted "ATTENTION!" and the line of pigeons halted instantly.

Sam gazed in awe at the line of pigeons that stood in front of him. Each one had broad shoulders, the proudest puffed out chest and feathers of the darkest, but shiniest grey Sam had ever seen. The backs of each of their necks gleamed with the richest deep purple and even their feet were the brightest pink, as if they had been polished to a perfect shine.

"Good afternoon gentlemen, ladies," the central pigeon spoke. "May I ask exactly what you are doing here? This is private property and strictly forbidden to outsiders."

"Please forgive us Sir," replied Mrs Major, "we've been travelling far and needed a safe place to rest for the evening. We didn't realise this place was private, we don't even know exactly where we are."

"Madame," spoke the grand looking pigeon, "we are the Royal Household Pigeons, my name is Corporal Frogmore and this," he gestured all around him with his gloriously preened wings, "is Buckingham Palace."

Mrs Major's beak hit the floor. In fact each and every one of them stood gobsmacked with beaks wide open. Mikey leaned over and whispered to Sam, "I wonder if he got his name like your Grandad Mad Frog?" both of them giggled quietly like naughty school pigeons.

"Our apologies corporal," said Charlie stepping forward. "My name is Charlie Major, this is my daughter Elizabeth," Lizzie shot her father a surprised glance hearing him not use her real name Lizzie; he continued regardless. "This is Mrs Jacqueline Hedges and her son Michael," pointing each of them out, Mrs Hedges even bowed when her name was introduced, "and finally, this young gentleman is my Grandson Samuel".

"But you can call me Sam," interrupted the young pigeon.

"As my daughter was saying," Charlie continued, not fazed by the interruption, "we are on a journey but it is great to hear that we are almost at our destination."

"Your destination?" asked Corporal Frogmore.

"Yes corporal," replied Charlie, "We are gathering in St James' Park tomorrow."

"St James' Park?" questioned the corporal, "why and who is gathering at St James' Park?"

“It’s a long story,” replied Charlie, and he began to tell the Royal pigeons all about the last week, he told them of Victoria Buildings, of the plan and of their journey to where they were now.

“Well you can count us in,” said Corporal Frogmore after Charlie had finished regaling them with his tale. “We consider it our duty to defend our kind and will proudly stand with you to regain your rightful home.” The line of the household pigeons then stood to attention saluting Charlie with their right wings. “Anything you need us to do, just ask,” continued the corporal, “and you must stay here for the evening. St James’ Park is just the other side of the palace, but you will be safer here under our guard.”

“Thank you corporal,” replied Charlie, “can I ask that you look after the young boys? We are not yet fully prepared for our plan and the ladies and I have some things to arrange. We must also get the message, of our plan out to as many pigeons in London as we can.”

"Of course," said the corporal. "I will make sure they are well fed". He turned to the pigeon on his left, "lieutenant! Fetch Holly," he ordered, the pigeon flew off in the direction of the palace. "I will also send out the brigade to the north and south to help you spread the message." With that he directed the remaining pigeons to fly over the wall and persuade as many pigeons as they could find to be at St James' Park tomorrow.

"Can I help with your other arrangements?" asked the corporal.

"We shall go alone", said Mrs Major, "we don't want to draw to much attention to ourselves, but can you suggest a place where we can find bags of rubbish?"

The Corporal looked confused. "Bags of rubbish?" he asked. Mrs Major nodded. "Well unfortunately we don't have any here, all our rubbish is either recycled or composted at The Prince of Wales' insistence. May I suggest Soho."

"Soho?" asked Mrs Hedges, "what and where is that?"

"If you fly over the northern wall," the corporal directed, "fly until you see a big stone arch and turn right; head down Oxford Street, a long straight street full of shops, and when you get to the crossing at the far end go straight across; then head for the bright neon lights. You won't miss it. Soho is where the humans go to eat, drink and dance at all hours of the day, you will find plenty of rubbish there I'm sure. Now here comes Holly; we will look after and feed the boys and will have a feast waiting for you when you get back. Good Luck."

Charlie and the ladies took to the air and flew north.

"Be good for the corporal," Mrs Major shouted back to the boys watching them from the ground and she disappeared over the wall, Mrs Hedges and her father by her side.

Back on the manicured lawn of the palace the lieutenant returned landing directly beside the corporal. "Holly is on her way" he said, turning and pointing towards the palace. There rushing across the lawn, with her short legs moving as fast as they would carry her, was Holly the Queen's favourite corgi.

Sam and Mikey watched as Holly approached. She had the most luxurious and well-groomed light red fur with a bright white underbelly and nose with the cutest black button tip. Her legs, although short were capped with white fur that she almost looked like she was wearing furry white boots. Her light red ears pricked constantly to attention, like two impressive triangles crowning her head.

"Good evening corporal" she said graciously, "how may One be of assistance?"

"We have some guests," replied the corporal gesturing towards the young pigeons, "and I wonder if we could get them something to eat from the Royal kitchens?"

Mikey's ears opened wide at the sound of food. But this was not going to be any food, he thought, this was going to be ROYAL food; and his beak began to moisten with anticipation.

“Of course” replied Holly. “May I suggest that you meet One in the kitchen court yard, in say, five minutes?”

“Affirmative” replied the corporal; Holly turned on her heels and ran back towards the palace as fast as those short legs could carry her.

Five minutes later Sam and Mikey were standing in the cobbled courtyard of the Buckingham Palace kitchens. Appearing through a flap at the bottom of a large white door came Holly carrying in her mouth a bulging red gingham cloth. She approached the expectant young pigeons and placed the parcel in front of them. As she released the ends of the cloth from her mouth they folded out in front of her forming a chequered blanket, and right in the centre was a pile of breads, the likes of which the boys had never seen.

“So we have sourdough, rosemary focaccia & the chef’s best wholemeal bread,” explained Holly, “One hopes you enjoy.”

"Thank you so much," said Mikey his beak full of the focaccia, "this is the best bread I have ever tasted."

"I'm so very pleased you like it," replied Holly, "but One shouldn't speak with One's beak full."

Mikey gulped down the remaining bread in his mouth and with a slight bow of his head replied, "Sorry ma'am," he then leant forward and pecked out a lump of the sourdough bread.

The two young pigeons fed like kings, making sure to leave plenty for when their mothers and Charlie returned. In between feasting they explained to Holly their reason for being in Buckingham Palace and about their adventures with the big white flying machines and the tube train.

"You sound like very brave boys," replied Holly, "and Sam how clever of you to rescue you grandad."

"He also rescued me from a plastic bag," piped up Mikey, who continued to regale Holly with the scene at the reservoir.

“So clever, my boy,” she replied, looking at Sam again. “Plastic bags are such a dangerous thing to us animals. I have often heard her Majesty taking about birds getting trapped in them, and even fish in the sea eating them, making them sick. She doesn’t understand why people still use them and frankly, neither do I. Well I am glad you are safe and well Mikey; it’s always good to have a best friend to look after One’s back, and it sounds like you have one of the best friends there is.”

“I do,” replied Mikey, turning to his friend and smiling, “the very best.”

“I shall bid you goodnight young sirs” announced Holly. “I must go and lay at the end of her Majesty’s bed to ensure it is warm for her feet when she retires for the evening.”

“Goodnight,” said Sam and Mikey together, “and thank you once again for the bread,” continued Mikey, “I shall never forget the best bread I have ever eaten.”

Holly smiled, nodded towards Corporal Frogmore and retreated back through the flap at the base of the door where she had appeared earlier.

“Right then chaps,” said the corporal, “I think we should get you guys settled in for the night and wait for your mothers to return. Follow me,” and he lead them to a large, white wooden bird house, big enough for several pigeons, nestled amongst the trees by the lake.

“I wonder how mum’s getting on?” Sam asked Mikey and he nestled into one of the many arched openings to the house.

CHAPTER 10: RAINBOWS AND RUBBISH

As Mrs Major flew over the wall she was shocked by the noise that invaded her ears. The sounds of the busy traffic and the chatter and shouts of all the humans rushing about their business seemed a world away from the peace and tranquillity of the palace lawn.

The three pigeons flew north as instructed along a wide busy road that skirted the edge of the huge green space they had seen previously. In no time at all they could spot the huge stone archway that the corporal had referred to and they came to rest on the very top, high above the pedestrians that walked down below.

“That way,” said Mrs Hedges, pointing off to the right. “That must be the shopping street; look it’s just as he described”.

“You’re right Jackie,” said Mrs Major, “let’s get moving as it’s starting to get dark.” She was right; the sun was way past its peak and was heading quickly towards the ground like a bright big ball falling to earth after being thrown in the air. The three took off and headed straight for Oxford Street, flying above the buildings to stay away from the pavements below which were still packed with people, all of which seemed to go into the buildings with nothing and come out holding lots and lots of bags. Humans really are strange, they all thought. Mrs Major spied the bags they were carrying but knew they weren't the size they needed, they needed something much bigger.

Looking down as they reached the crossing, they could see strange markings on the road making a big X. Mrs Major wondered if there was buried treasure underneath, she remembered the stories of the pirate parrot that her father used to tell her, X always marked the spot of the hidden treasure. She smiled to herself, when this was all over she would make sure her father told the story to Sam; she had always loved story time with her father, but that would have to wait.

"So straight ahead we go, and keep an eye out for the lights," said Mrs Major once again focused on the task at hand.

Only a short distance from the crossing off to the right they spotted lines of streets filled with light. The buildings seemed to be covered in signs of many different colours which glowed in the dusky light of the early evening. Some of them had humans sitting outside on tables and chairs, or standing in big huddled groups chatting and drinking. Further down the streets the lights seemed to get brighter and brighter and the far off noise of music hung in the air.

They headed down one of the streets to the right keeping their eyes peeled for what they were after. As they reached the end of the street the music was now much louder. They could see large groups of people spilling out of bars onto the street all drinking and chatting and oddly, thought Mrs Major, there were no females just men. As they looked around the streets at the crossroads they could see flashing neon lights above the entrances to the buildings and many of the windows were painted with the colours of the rainbow. As she looked down the street to her left, Mrs Major spotted an elegant red brick building with beautiful white trimmed bay windows protruding into the street on the first and second floors. At its base was what looked like another bar again with men crowded around its big glass windows and from inside came the sound of fun, lively music. Her eyes were suddenly drawn to the top of the building. Attached to the brickwork was a two metre long flagpole and beneath it hung a bright rainbow coloured flag, which billowed in the early evening breeze. It was not the flag however that had peaked her attention but the fact that standing on the end of the flagpole were two male pigeons. Apart from at Buckingham Palace these were the first pigeons they had seen and so the perfect opportunity to spread the plan further.

Mrs Major led the others over towards the building and they landed on the roof behind the flagpole.

In front, nearest to them, on the flagpole was a young pigeon; not as young as her son but definitely younger than herself. His neck was bright green, similar to hers, but then blended into purple and bright pink as it moved down to his chest; his head was more of a light blue than grey and with his piercing orange eyes he almost looked like the rainbow flag that flew beneath him. The pigeon behind him however, could not have looked more different. Slightly older this pigeon was almost completely black, like leather; except for a thin outline of grey on the tips of his wings that in the lights from the street shone like metal.

"Good evening gentlemen," Mrs Major introduced herself. "My name is Lizzie and this is my friend Jackie and my father Charlie. May we have a word?"

The two guys turned to each other and then towards Mrs Major. The rainbow coloured pigeon stepped forward and began to speak.

"Of course you can sweetie," he said, "my name is Dean and this is my partner Rupert." Behind him Rupert nodded in way of introduction. "I love your neck," Dean continued, "you look Fab-u-lous! How may we boys be of assistance to such a glamorous beauty?"

"Well," replied Mrs Major, "let me explain." She then began the whole story, which she had by now told to so many pigeons, that she didn't even have to think about what she was saying. Dean and Rupert seemed glued to every word.

"Oh my dear!" exclaimed Dean, once Mrs Major had finished regaling them of their trip and plan; "The drama of it all!"

"We absolutely will be there," interrupted Rupert poking his head out from behind Dean.

"We must ALL fight for what we believe in and stand up to the bullies and people who don't accept us for who we are. We will go and spread the word immediately," Rupert continued. "There are many who will believe like us, and we know exactly where to find them. I will go to Soho Square and tell the boys there and Dean, you find Karen and Gina and get them to tell all the girls." Mrs Major could see that Rupert had a real fire in his belly and they were both going to make a great difference to their plan.

"One last thing," asked Mrs Major, "is there anywhere nearby that we might find bags of rubbish? We were told this was the place to go."

"Absolutely," replied Dean as he pointed down the street. "Round that corner and look in the alleyways, you'll find exactly what you need I'm sure." Then bidding their farewells and promising to see them in St James' Park the following day, the two pigeons flew off; Rupert disappearing almost instantly as his black feathers blended with the night sky.

Following Dean's advice the three pigeons flew around the corner to a quieter street. The buildings on this street seemed to contain small shops and cafes which were closed for the evening. As Dean had described alleyways lead off from the street, they appeared dark, lit only by the lampposts in the street. On the corner of one particular alleyway they spied a closed bakery, its window filled with cakes and tarts and from the alleyway, spilling onto the pavement were black rubbish backs filled to the brim.

"That's exactly what we need," said Mrs Major, as they flew down and stood at the entrance to the alleyway.

As they stepped into the alley and surveyed their surroundings they could see that not only were there several black bags of rubbish, but that the gutter was filled with empty glass bottles, crisp packets and pages of newspaper.

"This is disgusting," said Mrs Hedges. "The humans have made such a mess and have the nerve to call us vermin." She turned to Charlie and Lizzie. "How can they do this and still call us flying rats?"

"You should take that as a compliment." Said a mysterious voice in the darkness of the alley, surprising the three pigeons who started peering into the dark alley looking for the owner of the voice. "Rats are noble and clever creatures," said the voice and it was at that moment Mrs Hedges saw two eyes peering back at her between the rubbish bags.

Mrs Hedges stood rooted to the spot in fear as the eyes grew bigger and bigger.

"Hello, my name is Murray," said the voice, which actually sounded extremely posh and they could all now see belonged to the rat that was poking its head through the gap between the bin bags; and he was smiling. "I don't get many visitors to these parts; it's an absolute pleasure to meet you."

The pigeons stood there in stunned silence. This was a very polite rat and not what they had expected from the ominous sounding voice in the dark.

“I’m....I’m....I’m sorry,” said Mrs Hedges still catching her breath from the surprise. “I didn’t mean to cause offence by what I said.”

“Don’t worry my dear lady,” replied Murray, “it’s completely understandable considering the bad press we get; but you’d know all about that too I should imagine,” and he chuckled. “May I offer you some refreshment or a bite to eat?” he asked.

“Oh, no thank you sir,” interjected Mrs Major, “we must be getting back to our sons, but we do have an important question to ask.”

“Well go ahead my dear girl” replied Murray. “Time and tide waits for no pigeon.”

Slightly confused by what he just said Mrs Major continued. “We need to get hold of one of these big black bags. Would you be able to help us?” she asked.

“Well I’m sorry my dear” replied Murray, “but as strong and brave as I may be; the Othello of the rat world no less, I would not be strong enough to lift one of these big bags as I am sure neither are any of you."

"No, no. You misunderstand sir" said Mrs Major, "I mean an empty black bin bag."

Murray began to laugh, a big booming laugh that seemed so out of place on a creature of his size. Seeing the puzzlement on his guests faces Murray stopped.

"My apologies to you all," he spoke eloquently, "I do have a flair for the dramatic. I spend most of my evenings sneaking into the theatres of these parts and I think all the Shakespeare has rubbed off on me."

Charlie looked at the rat's fur and couldn't see anything that looked like it had rubbed on to him. He definitely was an odd creature, he thought.

"Do not worry Sir Murray," replied Mrs Major, "please let me explain" and for the second time that evening she told the pigeon's tale.

"So you mean to catch this dastardly Hawk in one of these bags?" asked Murray thinking he had understood this elaborate plot. "Just like young Mikey was trapped in the bag at the reservoir?" he looked to Mrs Major for confirmation.

"Exactly," answered Mrs Major, "and then we'll be free to return to our real home."

"Well my dear," he replied, "this sounds like the most inspiring tale, a Henry the fifth or King Lear for our time." Again the pigeons looked confused. "Of course I shall play my part," he continued. "Wait right here, I will be back forthwith," and he scurried off into the darkness.

"Well he's just a bit crazy," said Charlie, "What on earth was he going on about?"

"I like him," said Mrs Major forcefully to her father, "and he's going to help us which is far more important. So be nice; and there's nothing wrong with a being a little bit eccentric, is there, Mad Frog?" She winked at her father.

About five minutes later Murray appeared again through the gap in the bin bags and this time carrying in his mouth was a neatly folded black bin bag, the size of a small envelope. He placed it down in front of Mrs Major.

“I know exactly where the baker keeps everything,” said Murray; “he still can’t understand how his strawberries go missing,” he giggled. “I do have one question,” he asked Mrs Major. “How do you intend to take this bag with you? Surely if you fly with it in your beak it will unwrap and cause you to fall?”

Mrs Major looked straight back at him, her eyes opened wide. She then turned to her father and Mrs Hedges looking for guidance or answers but they just looked right back.

“I hadn’t thought,” she said, “how stupid of me. This is not going to work and we shouldn’t have started this foolish journey,” and she started to cry.

“My dear, my dear,” said Murray softly as he walked up beside her. “You are a strong, independent lady, who by the sounds of things has raised a strong, brave independent son, and you will complete your mission because I’m going to help.”

Mrs Major's head jolted up, her eyes still full of tears. "What?" she said softly.

"I am going to help," said Murray confidently. "Let me know what time you need the bag for, and I will be at Trafalgar Square waiting for you."

"Really?" she asked, "You'd do that for us?" and she opened her wings and gave him the biggest of hugs.

"Of course my dear," replied Murray, "us rats, whether we fly or not, must stick together," and he looked her right in the eyes and smiled.

So the pigeons and the rat made a plan to meet in two days' time and then returned to Buckingham Palace.

Tomorrow was going to be a very big day, thought Mrs Major. A very big day.

CHAPTER 11: A STRANGE VIEW FROM THE WINDOW

In the gardens of Buckingham Palace, Sam and Mikey were stirring from there sleep in the bird house, as Mrs Major and Mrs Hedges were laying out breakfast which Holly had kindly brought them earlier that morning.

"Right then boys," announced Mrs Hedges, "breakfast is ready, freshly baked croissant for everyone."

The ladies were joined by the boys and Charlie arrived shortly after. He had been speaking with The Royal Household Pigeons. They would be unable to join them today on their short journey to the park, but would send one representative; the rest would be there the following day to support them on their return to Trafalgar Square.

"Right then boys, eat up," said Mrs Hedges. "Today's going to be a long day and there won't be food like this in the park, so make sure you fill up."

Not one to argue when it came to food, Mikey obliged and began to peck at the, still warm, croissant that flaked into pieces as he pecked, making it much easier to eat. Sam, Charlie and the ladies all joined him round the big, buttery pastry and began to eat.

As they finished eating they were joined by Corporal Frogmore.

“It’s a very short trip for you today” said the corporal. “All you need to do is fly over to the front of the palace, past the statue of the human with wings and down the red road. The park is on your right and hopefully they’ll be pigeons to meet you.”

“They will be there,” said Sam adamantly, “the message has gone out and they will come; won’t they?” his confidence dipped slightly and he looked to his Mother and Grandad for encouragement.

“We’ve done all we can do,” his Mother replied, “now we just have to believe and hope,” and she began to tidy the table, brushing the few remaining crumbs of croissant on to the ground with her tail feathers.

"Even if no one else comes," said Charlie, looking his grandson straight in the eyes, "we've seen it through and come so far, and you should be very proud of what you've done."

"The Royal Household Pigeons and I will definitely be there," he told Sam, "so you won't be alone," and he gave the young pigeon a wink.

It was the moment of truth. The time had come for them to depart and see if everything they had done, all the birds they had told of their plan, all the dangers they had encountered on their journey, had they all been worth it. They said their goodbyes to Corporal Frogmore and in a flurry of feathers took to the sky once more. They headed straight to the palace roof and landed to look out over their surroundings. Above their heads flying majestically in the wind was a flag; which Sam noticed was covered in strange red and gold animals, or monsters, he couldn't quite tell; they certainly looked fierce he thought. Out ahead of them Sam and Mikey were stunned by the view. They could see the monument which the corporal had described, topped with a gold winged human that glistened in the sunlight, but the most amazing part was the wide red road that stretched out in front of the palace. The young pigeons had seen nothing like it, it was as if someone had rolled out a giant red carpet in front of them, leading them to their new home, thought Sam. On each side of the road, all the way down, stood tall white flagpoles each holding a flag of red, white and blue.

The group of pigeons took off again, flying over the courtyard in front of the palace and the tall black iron fence that surrounded it. As they circled around the monument Sam could see that at the base of the monument was a statue of a large lady sat on a big chair. He looked up at the gleaming golden winged human and back down to this sitting lady and thought she looked rather grumpy and wondered why. He soon forgot about the grumpy lady when he looked down the road in front of him. Sam felt as if he was at the head of a grand parade with all the flags flying in front of him and started to fly down the big red carpet.

“This is St James’ Park” said Charlie pointing his wings to the right. “Clarence House is just up ahead, so keep a look out.” A short distance ahead Charlie started to descend, followed by the four others, he turned to the right to land in the park.

Staring out of a second floor window of Clarence House, Prince Charles looked puzzled. There seemed to be more pigeons than usual today, he thought to himself, as he saw five pigeons land in the park opposite. Looking down to the park opposite he shook his head in disbelief, as if to believe the image in front of him was some sort of dream, but no, there they were, just sitting opposite his house. How strange, he thought as he turned away from the window to leave the room to begin his day, there must have been over a hundred of them.

As Sam and the others came to land in the park, they couldn’t believe their eyes. The grass in front of them was barely visible, and rather than a sea of green there was a sea of grey. There must have been over a hundred pigeons on the ground in front of them. Looking for a place to land, Charlie spotted a cut tree trunk stump in the centre of the large mass of pigeons and led the others to it. Raised above the ground the five of them looked out in all directions at the wonderful sight, Mrs Major started to get very emotional.

"I can't believe it," said Mrs Major, holding back tears, "so many pigeons have come. You did it Sam. Your positivity made me believe in you, and it's made all these pigeons believe in you too. I am so proud of you."

"I think maybe someone should say something to them," said Charlie "and I think that someone should be you Sam," he continued turning to his grandson.

"Me?" asked Sam, quite shocked at what his Grandad had just said. "I couldn't possibly speak to all these pigeons, it should be a grown-up, that's who they'll listen to," he added.

"Nonsense," replied his Mother, "you're the reason they are all here. You said we should stand up to the bullies and get our home back and that's what these pigeons believe in too, so it's definitely you who should speak to them."

With that she flapped her wings to grab the attention of the crowd below and shouted out loudly.

"Good morning everyone," she started, "it's so wonderful to see you all here. For those of you who I haven't spoken to before, my name is Mrs Lizzie Major, and this is my son Sam," she pointed at her boy stood rigid next to her. "It was his idea and plan that we should not be living in fear away from our true home and that we should come here to take back our rightful home. If you wouldn't mind he would like to say a few words to you all." She stepped to one side and with a gentle nudge of her wing pushed Sam forward.

Sam looked all the way around the tree stump at all the pigeons that now stood silently, looking at him, waiting for him to speak.

"Hello," Sam said timidly, overwhelmed by the crowd in front of him.

"I think you'll need to be a little louder than that," said his mother, smiling at him, "make sure they can hear you at the back".

Sam coughed, looked around and began again.

"Hello everyone," he shouted confidently, "my name is Sam, and I would like to thank you all for coming and for believing in my dream that we should return to Trafalgar Square." He paused, looking around the sea of faces for a reaction but they all just stared straight back waiting for him to continue. "I have never known Trafalgar Square, unlike many of you, and I only have the stories of my grandfather to know how wonderful a place it was; however, I do understand that no one should be bullied into leaving any place and people that they love. That is why I hoped, and now seeing all of your faces, believe, that we can stand up to these bullies and reclaim that which was taken away from us, so that I and all the young pigeons like me can get to experience the place and times that my grandfather and many of you already have." Sam began to hear coos of agreement coming from the crowd and see heads nodding all around him. "So tomorrow may be dangerous" he continued with strength in his voice, "it may be tough; but our home is worth fighting for and if we stick together and believe in each other, we will be victorious!" He took a deep intake of breath and held it. Once again there was silence and for a moment Sam wondered what he had said wrong; when out of the blue came the most enormous sound as every pigeon in the crowd below began to cheer. Pigeons cooed, flapped and clapped their wings and jumped up and down in the air; and Sam breathed out in relief. As the noise began to calm down Sam raised both his wings and began to flap them lower and lower to the ground trying to get silence to descend again.

Now able to be heard again he continued, "I will now let my Grandad tell you a little of the plan for tomorrow and we will then come round and speak to all of you and discuss it."

Sam stepped back next to his mother, who gave him a big hug as Charlie stepped forward and began to address the crowd.

"Mum," said Sam, turning towards her.

"Yes son," she replied.

"Before we get all caught up in the plan for tomorrow" Sam continued, "can you take me to see the daffodils?" and he looked at his mother with wide eyes and his beautiful smile.

"Of course I will son," she replied, "come with me"; and she took off in the direction of Horse Guards Parade followed swiftly by Sam.

The pair of them arrived at the far end of St James' park a short while later, across the road Sam could see a big gravel covered square, surrounded on three sides by grand looking white buildings. Straight ahead in the middle of the building were three small archways above which stood an elegant clock tower and there, to the right of the tower he spied the enormous round wheel that he had spied looking so small from the crazy ladies balcony at Victoria Buildings. He couldn't believe how big it looked in relation to the buildings in front of him.

"Look mum," he exclaimed, "the London Eye! Look how big it is."

Mrs Major looked over to where her son was pointing, but she wasn't really looking at the big wheel. She was instead transported back to all those years ago when she had met Sam's father who had been wandering in Horse Guards Parade and spotted her in the park opposite and had flown over and introduced himself to her. Most of the males she had met previously always commented on her glistening emerald neck, but Isaac had been different and had complimented her eyes. She fell in love with him almost instantly. It helped that he was a fine figure of a pigeon. Extremely handsome his dark grey head and neck stood out on top of his broad chest which rather than being grey was almost white with just the tips of his feathers returning to the same dark colour as his head. He then took her and showed her the most beautiful part of the park filled with yellow daffodils and they had walked and talked all afternoon among the colourful flowers. After that afternoon they had hardly ever been parted until that fateful day in Trafalgar Square.

Sam spotted a single tear fall from his Mum's eye.

"Is everything ok?" he asked hopping over to his Mother.

"Yes, son," she replied, "just happy memories remembering your father, this is where we first met." And quickly changing the subject she continued, "let's go and see the daffodils, they are just over there, past the cottage."

The mother and son now flew along the side of a small lake in front of which stood a small rustic cottage. A few moments further down the path and Sam could see a small area of grass, edged with trees, and it was full of bright yellow daffodils. They landed in amongst the flowers, the sunshine hitting the yellow petals.

Sam looked at his feathers which seemed to turn yellow in the glow from the flowers.

"This place is beautiful" said Sam, "I can see why you liked it so much. Is Grandad right that Dad used to bring you the flowers when you were pregnant?"

"Yes he did," replied Mrs Major, "I couldn't fly here, so he brought the flowers to me instead. He was always so thoughtful and kind." She smiled at her boy seeing her husband's eyes in his. Her gaze was distracted by a dark shadow passing in front of the sun and then the burst of sunlight returning.

"Can you tell me more about him?" Sam asked his Mother.

"What would you like to know?" she asked back, again disturbed by a shadow passing in front of the sun and the flash of light following. "What is that?" she asked looking up into the sky. "Where were we? What did you want to know darling?" she looked back towards Sam.

“I want to know everything!” said Sam excitedly. “Am I like him?”

Mrs Major smiled and began, “well you have his eyes, and definitely his sense of adventure and he was very, very brave, just like you and…” once again she was cast into darkness, however this time the sun did not return. Puzzled she looked up to see the black shadow of a bird, it’s large wings outstretched and hovering above them and it seemed to be descending towards them. Mrs Major struggled to see what it was; the bright sunshine behind the creature blurred its edges and made the whole thing just look like a big, black, bird-shaped silhouette.

Mrs Major rushed in front of her son to protect him as this dark shadow descended closer. Only as it got closer to the ground and its angle to the sun changed could she begin to see clearer. A flash of white and Mrs Major froze on the spot digging her claws into the earth beneath her.

"It can't be!" she exclaimed. "I can't…." and words failed her. Sam was suddenly worried at what could possibly have shocked his mother in this way and was just about to fly off to get help when the bird landed. Sam was unable to see past his mother who was blocking his view. It was then he heard a strange voice say, "hello Lizzie" and it sounded friendly.

Mrs Major, her body still rooted to the spot, turned her head and looked at her son. She then turned her head back to the direction of the voice and replied, "Hello Isaac, is it really you?" and she ran to meet him wings outstretched. She would have recognised him anywhere and he hadn't changed a single bit. She closed her wings around him and hugged him never wanting to let him go again.

CHAPTER 12: SIT DOWN AND I'LL TELL YOU A STORY

"Sam, meet your Father," said Mrs Major turning round to see her son. "Isaac, meet Sam, your son."

Sam stared at the male pigeon standing in front of him, his white feathers shining in the sun. How could this be happening, he thought.

"How?" he asked tentatively, "You said dad had died."

"Well son," said Isaac, "It's a long story, but first things first, can I get a hug?"

Sam approached his Father slowly and nestled his head against his white chest feathers and Isaac wrapped his wings around the young pigeon.

"I never thought this day would come," said Isaac, still holding on tight to Sam, "I have been dreaming of this moment ever since I lost your mother all those years ago."

“But how did you lose her?” Sam asked and Mrs Major was thinking the exact same thing.

“Well let me tell you,” replied Isaac, “come sit down and I’ll tell you my story.” Mrs Major and Sam sat down between the bunches of daffodils and listened.

“Have you heard about the Battle of Trafalgar?” Isaac asked his son.

“Yes,” replied Sam, “It’s there that I thought you died helping Mum and Grandad escape”.

“Well, some of that is true,” Isaac continued, “but obviously you can see I’m very much alive and well.” He paused and smiled at them both, so happy to finally see them. “During the battle Harris, the hawk, was swooping down and attacking pigeons; he was being directed by a man wearing a large, funny looking, glove and they were trying to frighten us all away. Although there was only one hawk and many of us, Harris was just too quick and strong, with very sharp talons. I was trying to defend our home but I worried for your mother’s safety; so I convinced your Grandfather to get her to safety, while I tried to draw Harris away and give them time to escape. I just managed to see them hop into the back of an open topped truck when Harris swooped down and pinned me to the floor with his sharp talons. I was unable to move and could no longer see your Mother as one of the lions was blocking my view. Harris had my wings trapped but I pecked and pecked with my beak, stretching my neck as far as I could to try and get him off me and eventually I managed to pull out one of his chest feathers. He let go for a single moment and I flapped my wings as strong as I could, knocking him to the ground; I then flew and hid around the other side of the lion to try and catch my breath."

Sam looked at his father in wonder; how brave he was, he thought to himself. "And what happened next?" asked Sam impatiently.

"Well, I immediately looked for your Mother and the truck they had got on," Isaac continued, "but it was nowhere to be seen. Knowing they were safe from Harris I left the square and started to look for them, but

Trafalgar Square has many roads leading off from it and I had no idea where to start; so one by one I searched every road looking for the truck that had taken them to safety, but away from me." Isaac paused, beginning to feel upset at the reminder of losing them all those years ago but feeling overjoyed at the same time, having found them again. "I searched all night, and for the whole next week, but found no sign of them anywhere. So I decided that I would stay as close by as I could in the hope that they would someday return. Trafalgar Square was no longer safe, so I returned to Horse Guards Parade in the hope that being in the place where I first met your mother would lead me to seeing her again and it finally has."

"Oh my darling!" exclaimed Mrs Major, "I cannot believe that I've found you after all this time. The truck that we landed in didn't stop for hours after it left the square and I was unable to fly out and when it finally stopped we had no idea where we were and how to get back. The last thing I saw was the hawk dive into you with his talons and you fall to the floor and I presumed you had died. If I had ever known…" she started to cry.

"Don't cry, my darling," said Isaac, brushing the side of her face with his wing tip, "we are together now and that is all that matters."

"But how did you know we were here?" Sam asked his father.

"Well, my boy," he replied, "yesterday as I was resting in the parade I was surprised to be visited by a member of the Royal Household Pigeons as he flew by. He told me of a plan formed by a group of pigeons to retake Trafalgar Square and that I should meet in St James' Park today. When he told me the names of the pigeons that had landed in Buckingham Palace I couldn't believe what I was hearing. So when I saw you speaking to the crowd earlier and saw your Mother, I knew it was true and was overjoyed. I didn't know how to approach you so when I saw your Mother lead you here to the daffodils I knew that was my chance and now here we are, all together."

“You heard me speak this morning?” asked Sam, “that was so embarrassing, I was terrified.”

“Well I thought you were very brave,” replied Isaac, “and you’ve convinced me to help, we can’t let the bullies win, you’re absolutely right.” Sam smiled hearing his father’s approval.

“Talking of bullies,” interrupted Mrs Major. “Do you know if Harris is still in Trafalgar Square? It would help us to know before tomorrow,” she added.

“Not all the time,” answered Isaac. “Since all the pigeons left he is only brought back, by the gloved man, twice a week; but tomorrow is Sunday, so he’ll definitely be there.”

“Well then we better go back and tell the others,” said Mrs Major, “let’s get this plan moving. My father is going to be so shocked and happy to see you.”

With that, the family of three pigeons left the daffodils, and flew back to the waiting crowd where Charlie had just finished speaking.

After getting over the initial shock, Charlie hugged his son-in-law, and listened to the story of how he had come to be there. They also informed him that Harris was going to be in Trafalgar Square tomorrow, so they would have to be full on organised.

"Right then!" announced Charlie, "let's get organised and let everyone know."

So the now group of six gathered round and formulated their plan. They then split up and headed out into the crowd to inform the mass of pigeons.

As Mrs Major headed out into the crowd she came across Dean and Rupert, whom she had met the previous night.

"Morning Lizzie," said Rupert, "may I introduce our friends?" Behind Rupert stood a group of twenty young male pigeons and to his left next to Dean an equal sized group of females. "This is Karen and Gina," introduced Rupert, pointing to two short pigeons standing at the front of the female group. "They brought all these lovely ladies to help tomorrow," he continued.

"Hello ladies," said Mrs Major, "It's great to have you with us. Shall I tell you how you can all help?"

"The pleasure is ours," said Karen introducing herself, "anything we can do just let us know. Gina here is a dab hand at treating and repairing damaged feathers should it come in handy, as are some of the others."

"That's fantastic," replied Mrs Major, "in that case I'll suggest any of the pigeons able to nurse wounds form a separate group who we'll keep in back-up to help any injured pigeons." Gina called to the groups telling any trained pigeons to follow her and she flew to a clear area of grass nearby followed by a group of twelve mixed from the two groups of boys and girls. "The rest of you," continued Mrs Major, "we would like to form a group at the North West corner of the square in front of the

National Gallery. The plan is to confuse Harris the hawk with too many groups with him to cover," she explained.

"We'll create a demonstration to startle his eyes," exclaimed Dean, whose colourful neck feathers glimmered even more like a rainbow in the summer sun compared to the dark of the previous night. "We'll create so much noise and colour in that corner, he won't know what's hit him" he carried on, a sense of Pride in his voice and a cheer went up from the remaining pigeons behind them.

"Excellent" replied Mrs Major. "I will leave you to plan. We will regroup in the morning and return to Trafalgar Square at Midday," and again the group cheered.

Meanwhile Mrs Hedges, accompanied by Mikey, had found the group of pigeons from the areas around Victoria Buildings that Lizzie and herself had spoken to the days before they left.

"Thank you so much for coming," said Mrs Hedges, "we hope your journey was uneventful unlike ours," and she told the group of their eventful journey. She continued to outline the plan to confuse Harris the hawk and that they should form a group in the South West corner of the Square, in front of the left fountain as you looked towards the National Gallery. "If you can draw Harris as close to the fountain as possible and try and get him as wet as possible, by any means necessary," she added. The pigeons all nodded and when she informed them that they attacked at midday they all started to cheer.

Charlie had sought out the representative of The Royal Household Pigeons amongst the crowd. He was quite easy to find, being the tallest and strongest looking pigeon in the crowd by far, along with his tell-tale purple strip on the back of his neck.

"Good afternoon lieutenant are these your volunteers?" asked Charlie, approaching the Royal Pigeon and gesturing to the group of pigeons surrounding him.

"Yes Sir!" shouted the lieutenant, "all present and correct, Sir!" The pigeons had been recruited to the cause the previous evening by the Royal Pigeons set out on their mission by Corporal Frogmore.

"Superb," replied Charlie, "Welcome," as he nodded to the group of around thirty pigeons.

"What are our orders Sir!?" asked the lieutenant, who was unable to do low volume, thought Charlie.

Charlie firstly addressed the civilian pigeons. "Ladies and gentlemen, we would ask you to take up position in the South East corner of the square and create a distraction for Harris the hawk. May I suggest you use the water of the right fountain, soak his wings as much as you can and if you can get it in his eyes, even better." He continued to explain how the bin bag would be used to capture the hawk but they needed him as disorientated as possible to make it happen. He then turned to the lieutenant and continued, "lieutenant, I would ask you and the rest of the Royal Household to take position at the very top of Nelson's Column. From there you can oversee the whole square and come to the assistance of whichever group or individuals need support. Please tell the corporal we have a special mission for him which we will brief him on tomorrow."

"Understood Sir!" replied the lieutenant, "I will inform the others immediately! Permission to be dismissed Sir!"

Before the lieutenant flew off Charlie informed them all that they should be in the park the following morning ready to advance on Trafalgar Square at midday sharp and once again a cheer filled the air of St James' Park and the Royal pigeon took off in the direction of the palace.

As all the pigeons began to put their own plans together in their separate groups Sam and his father had found a quiet spot on the wall of Clarence House to discuss the key part of the plan.

Sam explained to his father how Mikey had been caught in the plastic bag at the reservoir and how by grabbing the handles from each side they were able to open the bag for Mikey to escape.

"The plan," Sam told his Dad, "is for two strong pigeons to fly, holding a handle each, and catch Harris in the bag. Corporal Frogmore will hold one side and I think you would be perfect to hold the other."

"Do we have a bag?" asked Isaac, "and what do you plan to do with Harris once you've captured him?"

"Mum has arranged for a rat to bring us a big, strong black bag," explained Sam to his father, "and I've had an idea about what we can do with Harris which I think might just work and mean we'll never have to worry about him again, but we can come to that later. First we need to work out how we can sneak up on Harris with such a big bag."

"I think I can help there," replied Isaac. "If the corporal and I hide among the columns of the church in the North East corner, when he flies down from his perch on top of The National Gallery, we should be able to sneak up behind him and catch him."

"That sounds perfect," agreed Sam, "we can run it past the corporal tomorrow but I'm sure it will work," and he leaned over and hugged his father.

Lizzie, Jackie, Charlie, Isaac, Sam and Mikey once again met up on the chopped tree trunk and surveyed the crowds of pigeons.

"Right then everybody," shouted Sam to the crowd confidently "we will see you all tomorrow and at midday we TAKE BACK OUR HOME," the crowd cheered and scattered around the park to look for food and places to rest.

Moments later Prince Charles appeared at the same second floor window of Clarence House as earlier and looked out at the park. To his surprise it was completely empty and he could see nothing but grass and trees. Maybe he did imagine it, he thought and he moved back away from the window.

CHAPTER 13: HARRIS

Early on the Sunday morning, a dark green 4x4 pulled up at the edge of Trafalgar Square. The driver's door opened, and out stepped a man in a tweed jacket and matching flat cap. He walked around to the rear of the vehicle and opened the back door. Leaning forward he picked up a large leather glove which he placed on his right hand. The large five fingered glove seemed to triple the size of the man's hand and covered all the way down to his elbow. Leaning further into the vehicle he emerged with his right arm outstretched on which stood a giant hawk. The hawk gripped to the glove with two bright yellow claws, each made up of four razor sharp talons, three at the front like toes and one facing rearwards to keep balance.

Harris, the hawk, was infamous. In the past he had appeared on television and in newspapers which told of his daring mission to scare the pigeons from Trafalgar Square; now he was older and although he was still as fast as his younger days he was far less busy with his work and spent most of his time sat on top of the National Gallery keeping watch for trouble.

The tweed wearing man removed a small hat from Harris' head, which had been covering his eyes so he could sleep on the journey from his home in Kent; he then pushed his arm upwards and Harris loosening his grip, unfurled his wings and took to the sky in a flourish. Harris' wings were huge, nearly a metre and a half in length from tip to tip; dark brown in colour with reddish coloured shoulders. As he soured into the sky his dark tail feathers fanned out behind him coloured white at both their tips and the base. He circled the square looking down for any intruders with his black beady eyes. All was quiet and after completing one more circle of the square he came to rest on a corner of the National Gallery opposite a church and kept watch.

Harris knew it wouldn't be a busy day. Two times a week, every week for the last however many years, he had been there and nothing eventful had ever happened; so why should today be any different, he thought, and he let his mind wonder.

Harris now led a lonely life; his only companion was his tweed wearing master. He remembered happier times in his past, long before he had ever been to Trafalgar Square. He lived in the grounds of some castle ruins, surrounded by a moat, in the countryside of Kent, with grass and trees everywhere. There, groups of people would watch him as he flew about the main lawn, performing aerial stunts for their amusement. He would be placed on the gloved arms of human children who would look at him with wonder and stroke his glossy feathers.

It had all changed for Harris after this master had had a meeting with a group of men in dark, black suits. They had arrived at the castle ruins in long, big, black cars with blacked out windows. These men had talked with his master for some time and before leaving, handed him a suitcase; when his master opened the case Harris could see it was full of banknotes.

The very next day Harris had been woken early and placed in the masters 4x4 wearing his special hood. When it had been removed, the green grass and trees of Kent had gone and been replaced by the concrete ground and tall buildings of the city. His master then got him to perform his aerial routines, but instead of for children he was flying directly into crowds of pigeons.

The pigeons would fly away scared; no wonder, Harris thought, because his body and wingspan were almost double the size of theirs and his sharp talons would scratch them if they got too close.

Each time he scared the pigeons his master would reward him with treats and he soon realised that the more he scared the small birds, the more treats he would get. He became more and more scary and started using more and more elaborate flying routines.

The humans began to come and watch him at his work, just like at the castle. He was interviewed, with lights and cameras and he even saw his face in newspapers on the newsstand at the corner of the Square. Harris began to love this new work and the fame soon went to his head. He loved this interaction with people just like at the castle.

Then one day, after a particularly fierce days flying the day before, he arrived at the Square and the pigeons had all gone. His master stopped giving him treats and the people no longer came to watch. His visits to the city were cut to only twice a week, and he rarely scared anything anymore; just the odd pigeon or small bird who wondered into the Square by accident.

Now his flash with fame had disappeared, he sat alone watching the people below taking photos of the Square, not him, rushing about with their daily lives; none of them even knowing he was there. But he was there, standing watch and he would be ready to strike at a moment's notice.

CHAPTER 14: THE BATTLE FOR THE SQUARE

As the pigeons began to gather in the park on that fateful Sunday morning, Sam was so impressed to see how busy they had all been in preparation. He could see that they had been gathering items to help with the plan and he had an overwhelming sense of pride in them all for the efforts they had made.

As he sat with his Mother, Father and Grandad he already knew he was the luckiest pigeon alive as he had his family with him and soon he thought, they would have the perfect home.

They were soon joined by Mikey and Mrs Hedges and all back together, Mrs Major addressed them. “Right then gang” she said, “today’s the day when our journey comes to its climax.” She turned to Sam and Mikey. “Boys, you must promise me to stay clear of trouble. Stick with me Sam and you with your mother Mikey, and do whatever we ask of you. NO heroics” she warned firmly.

“Yes Mum, Yes Mrs Major” the young pigeons replied slightly disappointed.

"We'll need to make a final inspection of all the groups and make sure they are all clear on the plan and has anyone seen the corporal?" she asked.

"There he is," replied Mrs Hedges pointing to a group of large impressive looking pigeons landing in a far corner. She smiled and blushed slightly as she caught the corporal's eye.

"Sam, take your father to meet him," Mrs Major instructed, "and bring him up to date with his role with the bag."

"Yes mum," replied Sam; and he flew off with his father in the direction of the Royal Household Pigeons.

"Dad," Mrs Major continued, "you'll be in charge of the pigeons gathered from the North and South with the lieutenant; and Jacqui, you will lead the pigeons from Victoria Buildings and the West. Off you go and debrief them, and I'll take the Soho pigeons and the East."

All agreed they flew off to their waiting groups for final inspections. Midday would soon be here.

Gina and a group of the nursing pigeons had returned from a mission across the river heading over Westminster Bridge; they had snuck into the loading bay of St Thomas' Hospital and chanced upon an open delivery of bandages. Nicely rolled into tubes and light as a feather they had been easy for the pigeons to grasp in their claws and fly back to the park without the humans noticing. As they arrived back a second group was also returning having collected as many discarded lollypop sticks they could find.

"These will do perfectly," Gina said to Karen, we'll be able to patch up any wings and legs with these splints and bandages." She continued looking Karen straight in the eyes, "I don't want to see you anywhere near the field hospital, just you make sure you're careful," and she hugged her tightly. "You go off and join Dean and Rupert and I will see you on the other side of this, I've got work to do."

"Yes boss!" Karen replied making a joking salute with her right wing, "See you later I promise. I love you," and with that Karen flew off to join the Soho pigeons, leaving Gina busying herself with medical supplies.

Charlie had found his group over by the lake. Much to the displeasure of the resident ducks and geese, the pigeons were taking it in turns to practice their water splashing techniques on the lake, disturbing their peace.

"Great job everyone," called out Charlie, "but midday approaches and you should all dry off to be on top form from the start. There's a patch of sun over there, I suggest you all use it," and he pointed to a patch of sun across the path. The pigeons left the lake and followed Charlie's orders much to the pleasure of the local bird life.

Not far away Corporal Frogmore was inspecting his pigeons.

"At ease men!" he shouted as he saw Sam and Isaac approaching, "take over lieutenant," and he marched over to the approaching pigeons.

"Good morning gentlemen," said the corporal, "I believe you have a job for me?"

Sam and Isaac began to talk the Corporal through his role with the bag.

"You and I will hold the handles," explained Isaac, "and as the others distract him we sneak out from the church and capture him in the bag."

"Received and understood," said Corporal Frogmore, "but I do have one small problem I would like to raise." Sam and Isaac looked at each other puzzled. What could this be, they thought? "We don't have a bag," announced the corporal.

"It's on its way," said Sam confidently, although he had absolutely no idea if it was or not.

Little did Sam know however, was that he was right. At that moment, deep below Shaftesbury Avenue, Murray the rat, black bag in mouth, was rushing though the sewers undetected.

Having completed their inspections Charlie, Mrs Hedges, Mrs Major and Mikey joined Sam and Isaac with the corporal.

"Based on my previous experience," said the corporal to them all, "I think one last motivational speech to the troops would be appropriate."

They all looked to each other, wondering who would be the best candidate for this last, important speech.

"I've got this," said Isaac stepping forward "I know exactly what to say," and he flew to the cut-off tree stump while the others gathered the crowd.

Isaac stood on the tree stump and looked out at the crowd of pigeons. Each group stood before him, gathered together with their leaders standing at the front.

"Ladies and gentlemen," Isaac began, "the time has come for us to take back our home. It may be hard but if we work together we can be victorious." The crowd before him flapped their wings in agreement. "Like many of you," he continued, "I was there all those years ago when we were driven from our home and from our loved ones; back then we all did what was right for ourselves as individuals; we left with our families to protect them or flew of alone to protect ourselves. This was not wrong but by not acting together, by not being united it allowed Harris and his masters to win and take our home from us. But now we are back together, we have been reunited and by working together by standing united wing in wing, Harris will not beat us this time." Again the crowd flapped their wings and cheered. "We will all play our part in distracting Harris, but the most important thing we can do is STAND OUR GROUND!" he exclaimed. "Do not fly away; protect each other, protect our home and we will win. NOW LET'S DO THIS!" Once again the pigeons before him cooed with excitement and with hope of a better future and group by group they took to the air and flew down the park towards the square.

Leading the charge were the Soho pigeons lead by Mrs Major at the front, Sam glued to her side as ordered. As they approached Admiralty Arch at the end of the Mall, in the distance, they could hear Big Ben start to toll twelve. As the final bell sounded Mrs Major flew through the middle arch and entered Trafalgar Square.

As they crossed the busy road below them, they put their plan into action. The previous evening the Soho pigeons had gathered colourful strips of paper, tearing them from magazines and newspapers that had littered the streets; others had gathered flowers, everything from bright yellow daffodils to deep red roses and purple lavender. Now as they flew into the square heading for the furthest corner they began to wave and shake their feet and beaks and the colourful items they held. It looked like the entrance of a grand parade, a celebration of colour and they flew directly across the front on the National Gallery and landed in the North West corner of the Square.

As Harris sat on his perch on top of the National Gallery his attention was drawn off to the distance archway as what seemed like a rainbow flew through the central arch. He turned his head to investigate to see a riot of colour flying over the road towards him like nothing he had ever seen. As it turned left in front of him, he could see that this was no rainbow, but a mass of pigeons waving coloured items that billowed in the wind as they flew. He could not understand what was going on, but knew he now had a job to do and he positioned himself towards the edge of the building ready to take off.

"We've got his attention!" shouted Mrs Major down on the ground below. "Stay sharp!" she shouted to the group, "and keep waving those streamers."

"Here he comes!" shouted Sam, as Harris took to the air and headed straight for them. Sam had never seen anything so scary, as the huge winged bird dived towards them his sharp talons stretched out in front of him. As Harris got to within touching distance from the group of pigeons Rupert shouted "NOW!" and all of a sudden stems of flowers pushed into the air and into the flightpath of the approaching hawk.

Harris swerved immediately to avoid crashing into the flowers and losing his balance and climbed back into the air away from the pigeons. As he circled around the statue of Nelson, ready for another attack run, he couldn't believe what he saw in front of him. There was no mistaking it this time, thought Harris; no rainbow of colours to distract him. These were just pigeons; as he spotted Charlie flying through Admiralty Arch, followed by thirty pigeons.

By a strange coincidence, as the pigeons had entered the square, Mrs Vala, fresh from having her hair done, was passing in front of the museum, heading home to Victoria buildings. As she looked up at the strange sight before her, a big white bird poo fell from the sky and landed on her new shiny black hair, splattering everywhere. "Aaargh" she yelled, running to the tube entrance, "I really don't like pigeons." The rest of the humans, seeing a hawk circling above them, and the odd display of flower carrying pigeons, gathered their belongings and quickly crossed the roads out of the square where they stood and watched safely from a distance.

As Charlie and the pigeons entered the square they were immediately in position and he led his group down to the fountain in front of them. There they formed a line along one edge of the pool of water, standing on its curved concrete wall.

"He's on his way!" shouted Charlie to the line of pigeons, as he spotted Harris change direction towards them. "We've got to time this perfectly," he instructed the group. As Harris got closer Charlie held his nerve, the hawk was only metres away and moving at such a speed he would be on them in seconds.
"1...2...3...GO!" shouted Charlie as Harris reached the opposite edge of the pool. With that, the line of pigeons dove onto the top of the pool, scooping their wings into the water they threw them into the air sending upward showers of water straight into the path of the oncoming hawk.

Harris' vision was blurred by water droplets and with his feathers soaked through he was unable to manoeuvre back into the air. He came to rest on top of a lamppost across the road from the square and shook his feathers dry. Meanwhile Charlie and his group repositioned themselves on the other side of the fountain keeping a watchful eye on Harris' every move.

Unbeknownst to Harris, while he had been distracted by these groups, two male pigeons had secretly flown down the edge of Trafalgar Square and come to rest hidden behind the columns of St Martin in the Fields church in the corner of the square. There they stood hidden from view, waiting for their equipment to arrive. They had only been noticed by one human woman who had been sitting on the steps of the church in her overcoat wearing a strange oversized brimmed hat. She had looked at them and smiled but then quickly left, walking away from them towards a small parade of shops one of which she entered. As Isaac and the Corporal watched her disappear inside they noticed scurrying up the gutter in the road a rat, barely visible behind a folded black bag it held in its mouth.

"You must be Murray?" asked Isaac as the rat arrived at their feet.

"At your service," replied the rat, as he dropped the bag at their feet. Murray then helped the two pigeons unwrap the bin bag placing the two handles out in front which Isaac and the Corporal then stood beside. They were ready. All they needed now was the right moment.

As Harris' eyes cleared he could see that a third group of pigeons had positioned themselves on the ground around the furthest fountain. He had not noticed Mrs Hedges and Mikey lead their group of pigeons into position while he was recovering on the lamppost. He surveyed the scene before him; three groups of pigeons he would have to scare away, but which one first, he thought. Having initially failed with his first two attacks he decided to attack the newest group who had not seemed to have protected themselves by the water or with flowers. With a final shake of his wings he took to the sky and headed across the road and towards the far side of the square.

"Stay close," Mrs Hedges turned and said to her son, "stick behind me," and Mikey huddled in behind his mother's tail feathers.

From high in the air Harris could see the pigeons beaks were empty and were not gripping anything in their claws and so he commenced his attack, diving towards them talons outstretched, eyes fixed on the centre of the group. He was caught completely unaware and blinded by flashes of sunlight as he heard a pigeon shout "NOW!"

On hearing Mrs Hedges command, her group had bowed their heads and using their beaks picked up the flat coloured sheets they had been standing on. Harris had not noticed the flat pieces of crisp packets the pigeons had been standing on and now with their foil undersides revealed he was being blinded by sunlight reflecting from their surfaces. He continued to fly unable to see and he felt his feet graze the concrete steps as he headed up towards the National Gallery. He rounded the pillar and ploughed straight through the middle of the Soho pigeons like an out of control car. Pigeons were thrown to each side, and feathers flew into the air.

"Is everyone ok?" shouted Mrs Major to the crowd, split down the middle like a typhoon had just passed through. She called for the medics and soon Gina and a group of nurse pigeons had arrived and were patching and supporting wings. Luckily there had been no serious injuries and Gina was able to lead the injured away from the scene and to an area of safety back towards the park. Meanwhile Harris fighting to see through the white balls of light blurring his vision headed back to the roof of the Gallery and his perch. What was going on, he wondered, why were the pigeons not flying away and what were all these tricks they were using. He gathered his thoughts; he was going to have to step it up a gear.

Back down by the church Isaac turned to the corporal. "Now's our chance," he said, "when he makes his next dive he'll be heading away from us and we can fly up behind him and catch him."

"Agreed" said the corporal and they both grasped their handles and waited for Harris to move. So as Harris made this next dive towards the ground, Isaac and Corporal Frogmore lifted off from the church steps, the black bin bag billowing open behind them like a giant parachute.

Harris once again flew in the direction of Charlie and the fountain. Now aware of their plan he changed direction at the last minute as the birds jumped into the pool and circled back around. It was then that he spotted the bag flying towards him, held on each side by a pigeon. He pushed out his claws in front of him and aimed straight for them, hitting the corporal head-on, with his sharp talons.

The corporal released his grip from the bag and fell towards the ground injured, plunging into the pool of water below. He managed to pull himself to the surface with his wings but was unable to get out of the water. High from their perch on top of nelson's column the Royal Household Pigeons dove to the rescue pulling their corporal from the water and resting him safely behind one of the bronze lions. They sent for assistance and Gina arrived with bandages to wrap the corporal's injured chest.

Meanwhile up above Isaac was unable to control the bag which now kept floating in front of his face and he landed at the entrance to the gallery.

Harris, buoyed by this small victory flew round the base of Nelson's column and headed back towards the colourful pigeons in the North West corner. He knew the flowers were too weak to hurt him and he would not be caught by surprise this time.

"Stand your ground!" shouted Mrs Major as Harris headed for them, but before she knew what had happened Sam had taken to the air and was flying away from the group. "NO!" she screamed after him as Harris changed direction away from the group and after the young pigeon.

Sam had a plan. He flew as fast as he could and had drawn Harris away from the group, he reached his father with Harris just behind him and grabbed hold of the lose handle. “Take off!” he shouted to his father and they both had just left the ground as Harris headed straight towards them.

Harris barely managed to avoid the opening bag, brushing it with the white tips of his tail feathers as he shot straight up. As he turned towards the sky, his enormous wing struck Isaac who losing his grip on the bag was thrown to the side; rolling down the stairs to the Square’s lower level.

Seeing his friend in trouble Mikey took to the air immediately and flew straight towards Sam. Without stopping he swooped in and grabbed the lose handle flapping in the wind. The two boys now had control again and started to fly higher. Sam didn’t know how they were going to be able to catch the hawk now he knew of their plan. What they needed was a miracle. They searched the air for Harris waiting for him to attack again and there from the direction of the church they could see him heading their way. All of a sudden over Harris' shoulder, emerging from the bright ball of light of the sun Sam spotted a fleet of sparrows speeding towards them. He recognised them immediately, it was the sparrows from Barrowgate Road, and out in front was Ron. They over took Harris at speed and Ron shouted to Sam and Mikey.

"Right then kids!" he shouted, "let's catch this hawk and end this thing. Follow us!" The sparrows turned and flew in front of the two young pigeons. They quickly reached Harris and began to buzz around him like flies. Far quicker and more agile than Harris they swarmed around him and blocked his line of sight, weaving around him as if they were tying him in knots. Then as fast as they had appeared in front of him they disappeared and as he brought his eyes forward all he could see was black as he flew directly into the open bag.

As Harris hit the base of the bag at speed, Mikey and Sam let go and the handles closed in around him, flapping uncontrollably inside trying to escape, the bag hit the floor and Harris was knocked unconscious.

"We need to move fast!" Sam called to Mikey. "Help me grab the bag, and follow my lead." Struggling to lift the bag Sam directed them to the edge of the square and the road where he searched the traffic below.

"There," he said, pointing his beak in the direction of the road below. Stopped at the traffic lights Mikey could see an open topped truck with what looked like a picture of a green acorn and leaves on its bonnet.

"Let's go," said Mikey knowing exactly what his best friend had got planned, and they flew down and dropped the black bag into the rear of the truck. The lights turned green and the truck drove off, turning the corner and disappearing from sight.

“We did it!” said Sam turning to his best friend, “We actually did it” and they cheered and laughed as they flew back to the centre of the square.

All the pigeons had gathered in front of the National Gallery and as Sam and Mikey landed they whooped and cheered for the two young pigeons. Bursting through the crowd Mrs Major and Mrs Hedges ran up to their boys and hugged them.

“Is everyone ok?” Sam asked his mum, “where’s Dad?”

“Your Dad’s fine” replied Mrs Major “the corporal and the others are being looked after by the nurses and will all make a full recovery, all thanks to you boys.”

“You got us back our home,” said Charlie walking up the stairs behind them. They all turned to see Charlie helping Isaac, who was limping up the stairs.

"We all did it," replied Sam, "and we had some extra special help," and he looked towards the sparrows standing off to the left.

"See I told you they weren't bad lads," said Ron, "and we birds have got to stick together."

"Absolutely!" shouted Sam, and just at that moment the Soho pigeons threw all their coloured streamers into the air and they filled the sky like a ticker tape parade.

Off to the right, the lady from the church steps had entered the square, still wearing her overcoat and hat; but now she was carrying a bag of bread in her hand. Charlie recognised her immediately as she started to scatter lumps of bread at their feet. He flew over and rested on the brim of her hat which was full of pieces of bread. "Welcome home Mrs Bread," he whispered gently, "welcome home," and he smiled looking over towards his daughter with her husband and amazing young son.

Two hours later and many, many miles away Harris was woken with a jolt as the truck came to a stop. Still a little dizzy a few moments later his dark surroundings lightened as a man in a green waxed jacket pulled open the bag he was surprised to find in his truck.

"Well hello there," the man said to Harris, "who do we have here?" Harris jumped out of the bag onto the side of the truck where behind the man he could see a grand stately home and acres of grass and trees. The man looked Harris over and was unable to see any identity tags, so looked at him and said, "Since we don't know where you come from, maybe you'd like to live here with us? I am definitely sure, our visitors will love you, especially all the kids," and he gave Harris a smile. "Welcome to your new home".

THE END

Printed in Great Britain
by Amazon

41021896R00098